FORBIDDEN VOWS

A Dark Mafia Romance Written
in Blood and Ruin

Nolan Crest

Copyright © 2025 Nolan Crest

All rights reserved

The characters and events portrayed in this book are fictitious. Any similarity to real persons, living or dead, is coincidental and not intended by the author.

No part of this book may be reproduced, or stored in a retrieval system, or transmitted in any form or by any means, electronic, mechanical, photocopying, recording, or otherwise, without express written permission of the publisher.

Cover design by: Emily Harper
First Edition: 2025
Printed in the United States of America

Dedication

*For the ones who rose from the ash,
who loved like war and healed like fire.
This story is yours.
And mine.*

"Some women aren't made to be saved.
They are the storm, the blade, the vow whispered through clenched teeth."

NOLAN CREST

CONTENTS

Title Page
Copyright
Dedication
Epigraph
Author's Note   1
Preface   2
Prologue   4
Chapter 1   8
Chapter 2   13
Chapter 3   19
Chapter 4   25
Chapter 5   32
Chapter 6   36
Chapter 7   44
Chapter 8   53
Chapter 9   59
Chapter 10   64
Chapter 11   69
Chapter 12   76
Chapter 13   81
Chapter 14   86

Chapter 15	90
Chapter 16	97
Chapter 17	101
Chapter 18	106
Chapter 19	112
Chapter 20	116
Chapter 21	122
Chapter 22	126
Chapter 23	134
Chapter 24	140
Chapter 25	144
Chapter 26	150
Chapter 27	155
Chapter 28	161
Chapter 29	165
Chapter 30	171
Epilogue	175
Afterword	179
About The Author	181
Books By This Author	183

AUTHOR'S NOTE

Dear Reader,

I wrote *Forbidden Vows* with my heart racing and my hands shaking—because this story demanded to be told loud, bold, and bloody.

This is for the women who were told they were too much. Too loud. Too dangerous. Too emotional. Too fierce to ever be loved right.

Valentina Russo is all of that and more—and she doesn't shrink for anyone. She's not a damsel. She's not a pawn. She is the storm.

And Damien? He's the man who dares to stand beside her, not above her. A king who knows real power comes when you *choose* each other—even in the shadows.

This book is full of knives and kisses, betrayal and tenderness, power plays and poetry. It's about rising from ruin. About what love looks like when it's *earned through fire*.

If you're here for spice, for sharp dialogue, for lovers who burn and break and still choose each other—you're in the right place.

Let's burn it all down,
Nolan Crest

PREFACE

They say you can't outrun your blood.

I tried.
I buried my name. Burned my fingerprints. Vanished into smoke and silence.
But blood remembers.
And the past? It never stays dead. Not when it wears your father's face.

I was born Valentina Russo—daughter of a king who built his throne from bones and betrayal.
In my world, love was a luxury. Loyalty was currency.
And power? Power was the only god we ever learned to worship.

My mother died with secrets in her throat. My father buried her with a kiss and a warning. I was told never to ask why.

So I didn't ask.
I *watched*. I *learned*. I bled.
Then I ran.

Years passed, and I thought I had escaped. Until I left a mark —a single blood-smeared Queen of Spades—on the ashes of a Syndicate lab. And just like that, I was pulled back into the underworld I once fled.

That's when he came for me.

Damien Moreau.

He is the knife beneath silk. The silence before the kill. The storm that does not shout—but still destroys everything in its

path.
He didn't flinch when he found me. Didn't blink when he bound me. Didn't care that I wasn't afraid.

He saw me.
Not as a daughter. Not as a pawn.
But as a threat. A mirror. A fire to match his own.

We were supposed to be enemies.
He was vengeance wrapped in a tailored suit. I was rebellion dressed in leather and scars.
He needed information. I wanted freedom.
But somewhere between secrets and seduction, between betrayals and bloodshed... something else was born.

Not love. Not yet.
Something darker.
Need. Hunger. Recognition.
A promise neither of us made, but both of us would kill to keep.

This is not a love story.
It's a story of war—of knives against throats and lips pressed against danger.
Of two people destined to destroy each other... or burn the world to build something new.

If you're looking for a gentle romance—close this book now.
If you want clean kisses and tidy endings—you won't find them here.

But if you're ready to fall into the fire...
Welcome to the underworld.

I'll be your guide.

— *Valentina Russo*

PROLOGUE

- Queen of Spades -

BLOOD STREAKED THE CONCRETE like brushstrokes of violence.
The air reeked of cordite and betrayal. Gunfire cracked through the night like thunder through bone. Somewhere, someone screamed—and then went silent.

Damien Moreau didn't flinch.

He moved through the shadows like a storm in silk—sharp suit soaked at the cuffs, jaw clenched so tight it ached. His Glock was warm in his hand, its magazine already half-spent.

The warehouse loomed around him, a cathedral of chaos—flickering fluorescents, overturned crates, the scent of burning chemicals rising like incense to some unholy god.

He kicked down the side door, boots splashing through a puddle of blood.

"Domenico!" he shouted.

No answer.

Just the low, wet cough of someone dying.

And then he saw him.

Slumped against a stack of pallets, his brother—his blood—was cradling his side, crimson pouring between his fingers like spilled wine.

"No. No, no—" Damien dropped to his knees, pressing his hands to the wound. "Stay with me, *fratello*. You hear me?"

Domenico smiled, weak and crooked. "Took you long enough."

"You're gonna be fine," Damien lied.

"You always were the better liar," his brother rasped, coughing red.

And there—pinned to Domenico's chest with a blade through the collarbone—was a playing card.
A Queen of Spades.

Soaked. Blood-speckled. Mocking.

It was the same card they used as kids, during their secret games of war and kingdom. The Queen meant betrayal. It meant death.

Damien's stomach twisted.

"Who did this?" he whispered.

Domenico's eyes flickered. "Someone inside. Someone... trusted."

Damien heard footsteps—boots, fast and closing.

The Syndicate. Reinforcements. Too many to fight alone.

"I won't leave you," Damien said, fire rising in his throat.

"You already did," Domenico murmured. "But it's okay. You live. You find them."

More blood. Less breath.

His brother's hand trembled, reaching up. Damien caught it, clutched it tight—until the grip loosened.

Then failed.

Then fell.

Silence.

Just the hum of broken lights and the hollow thunder of approaching death.

Damien closed Domenico's eyes.

Then he took the card.

Flashback
Two boys, barefoot, running through vineyards in southern France.
Sunlight. Laughter. A pact cut into skin with a stolen knife: *"Always protect each other."*

Back to the now—Damien, heart like ice and fire, standing alone.

He ran.

Out through the side, bullets ricocheting behind him. Into the dark, the rain, the waiting silence of grief.

At the riverbank, he stopped.

Looked at the Queen of Spades one last time. The blood on it was dry. His hands were not.

He struck a match.

Held the card to the flame.

Watched it curl, blacken, and burn into nothing.

But the image never left him.

The queen. The blood. The betrayal.

For the sins of the fathers, the children bleed.

He lit a cigarette off the dying flame.

The river carried the ash away.

And deep in his chest, a promise began to grow like rot.

"One day, I'll find the one who left that card. And I'll watch them burn."

CHAPTER 1

- Smoke & Steel -

THE AIR TASTED LIKE metal and intent. Valentina Russo crouched on the rooftop, the wind slicing through her like a promise. She adjusted her gloves, black leather creaking as she pulled the mask over her face.

Below her, a Syndicate-run pharmaceutical facility pulsed with light and money—its secrets locked behind concrete and arrogance.

"Val, we're green. No movement on cams," Gia's voice crackled through the earpiece, smooth and calm. "You're ghosted."

Valentina didn't respond. She didn't need to.

She clipped in, braced herself, and rappelled down the face of the building like a phantom. No sound but her breath. No thoughts but the objective.

Inside the facility, two guards passed—one yawned. They never saw her coming.

One silenced dart. A knife between ribs. Bodies dropped like afterthoughts.

"Warehouse corridor is two left turns and a security scan. Ezra's running distraction now," Gia said.

A distant BOOM rattled the floor. Shouting.

"Found the chaos," Valentina whispered.

Ezra's voice chimed in, breathless with mischief. "You're welcome."

She moved like water—fluid, lethal. Each step closer to the vault wasn't just a mission.
It was retribution.

The Card and the Fire

The vault door was older than she'd expected. She pulled off her gloves, cracked her knuckles.

"Gia."

"Already inside the grid. Ten seconds."

A soft *whir*. Then: *click*.

Valentina exhaled.

Inside, crates of synthetic opioids stacked like gold bars. Enough poison to rot cities. This wasn't just black market—it was war fuel.

She pulled a small gas canister from her bag. Uncapped it.

Lit a match.

The flames leapt like they'd been waiting.

Behind her, the fire painted shadows of angels and monsters across the steel walls.

She reached into her jacket, pulled out the Queen of Spades—creased, blood-smeared, deliberate.

She placed it atop the highest stack. No words. Just a symbol.

Her calling card.

The one the Syndicate would never forget.

A flicker of memory hit her—*a body in a warehouse, a card pinned to a corpse, her brother's eyes dulling as the blood left him.*

Domenico.

For him, she didn't just burn buildings.
She burned *empires.*

Ashes and Aftermath

The night was a ribbon of black and flame behind them. The explosion still echoed in Valentina's bones as the getaway van tore down the mountain road—no headlights, tires screaming over cracked asphalt.

Inside, Ezra whooped from the front seat, face streaked with soot and blood.

"Did you *see* that shit?" he yelled over the rush of wind, head half out the window like a lunatic dog with a vendetta. "Boom, baby. That place lit up like New Year's in hell."

Valentina didn't reply. She sat in the back, silent, knuckles white where she gripped the metal edge of the bench seat.

Gia turned from the passenger side, her eyes scanning Valentina with surgical focus. "You okay?"

Valentina looked at her for a beat too long.

"I'm fine."

But she wasn't. Not really. Not inside.

Because she could still smell the fire.

Not the fire she set.
The one from *before.*
From the night everything changed.

She blinked, and for a moment, the van dissolved.

She was back in that goddamn warehouse. Blood soaking into her knees. A card pinned to her brother's chest. A promise made between clenched teeth and shivering rage: *They'll pay. Every last one of them.*

The memory licked at her heels like the flames behind them,

always chasing, never close enough to kill.

They reached the safehouse—a nondescript concrete cube outside Marseille, surrounded by dying vineyards and wild dogs.

Gia locked the perimeter with a swipe of her phone. Ezra leaned against the door, lighting a cigarette with a still-shaking hand.

Inside, it was dim. Quiet. Too quiet.

The kind of quiet where truth tends to bleed.

Valentina moved straight to the sink, the mask still clinging to her face like a second skin. Her fingers trembled only once as she pulled it off.

It hit the countertop with a soft thud—leather on steel.

She turned on the faucet, cold water roaring. Blood—*someone's, many someones*—ran in spirals down the drain.

Behind her, Gia sat on the arm of the couch, chewing her lip. Ezra dropped into the chair, one leg bouncing, his energy still ricocheting from the high.

"Tell me you left the card," Gia said again.

Valentina didn't speak.

She reached into her chest rig, pulled out a folded photo—old, worn, nearly torn at the edges.

Domenico.

Smiling. Arm slung around her shoulder. Pre-betrayal. Pre-blood.

She looked at it for a heartbeat too long.

Then slid it back inside her gear.

"I left it," she said quietly. "Let them know a storm's coming."

Ezra grinned. "Hell yeah."

Gia looked unconvinced, eyes narrowing. "You sure this isn't going too far?"

Valentina turned slowly, meeting her gaze with something ancient in her stare. Cold fire. A war-song written in silence.

"It's not far enough," she said. "Not yet."

In the bathroom mirror, she studied her reflection.

Soot smudged her jaw. A small nick above her eyebrow bled lazily. Her eyes—those ice-dark eyes—held no victory.

Just calculation.

She rinsed her face. Tied her hair back with a black silk ribbon. Dried her hands.

Then she opened a drawer beneath the sink. Pulled out another Queen of Spades. Unbloodied. Crisp.

She kissed it, leaving a crimson print.

Another card. Another promise.

Outside, thunder cracked.

Somewhere, a king was watching footage. Somewhere, the name *Russo* was being whispered like a curse.

Let them whisper.

Let them remember.

Valentina Russo was no longer just a daughter.
Not just a ghost.
Not a footnote in someone else's legacy.

She was the fuse.
And this was only the beginning.

CHAPTER 2

- The Card -

THE ROOM PULSED with silence.

A single security monitor flickered in the dark, casting faint blue light across the sleek interior of Damien Moreau's private office. The walls were glass, but no city lights touched him here. He liked it that way—untouched, unseen.

Onscreen, the footage played back in slow, grainy detail.

A figure dropped from the ceiling like a whisper sharpened into steel. Black leather. Masked. Efficient. Every movement was controlled—danger disguised as grace.

Damien's jaw tightened.

He didn't need sound to feel the precision of her takedowns. One guard down with a strike to the larynx. Another dragged into shadow. A third crumpled with a syringe to the neck.

Then she reached the vault. Set fire to the product. No hesitation.

And as the flames bloomed across the camera feed, she turned—just for a second—and placed something down on the scorched marble floor.

A playing card.

Queen of Spades.

Blood-smeared. Intentional.

Damien froze the frame. Stared at it.

Time slipped sideways.

The memories returned like they always did—uninvited, violent.

He was back in that warehouse.

Blood on his hands. Smoke choking the air.

Domenico lying in his arms, trying to speak through a throat full of blood. The light dying in his eyes.

And on his chest—

That same card.

Damien hadn't spoken a word that night. Not to the police. Not to the Syndicate. Not even to his father when the old man demanded retribution.

He had memorized every angle of that card.

The font. The stain. The way it was deliberately bent at the corner, like it had been held too tightly in a gloved hand.

Now here it was again, years later, dropped like a gauntlet in a burning building.

He sat back slowly, expression unreadable. But under the surface, fury bloomed like wildfire—hot, silent, all-consuming.

His fingers curled around the armrest of his leather chair. The wood beneath creaked. Then cracked.

A voice came over the intercom.

"Mr. Moreau, the Marseille lab was—"

"Silence," he said, softly. Deadly.

He stood and walked toward the window, hands clasped behind his back. Monaco's skyline glittered beneath him like a kingdom unaware of its own fragility.

He didn't turn when he spoke again.

"Find her," he said. "I don't care what it takes. Bring me the one who left that card."

A pause.

"And if she resists?"

"Then make her bleed," he murmured. "But not before she understands what she's ignited."

Fire in His Veins

He remained still long after the room emptied.

The silence wasn't peaceful—it pulsed. Thick. Heavy. Alive. The kind that fills a space after something has broken, and the pieces haven't hit the floor yet.

Damien stood by the window, a statue carved from control. Below, Monaco stretched out in cold city lights, glittering like something beautiful and breakable. From this height, everything seemed manageable. Even vengeance.

But this wasn't about management anymore. It wasn't about the business, the empire, or the rules of the underworld.

This was memory. This was personal.

He turned back toward the desk. The monitor still played the frozen image—her figure half-shadow, half-smoke. The woman in black. Moving like vengeance given form.

There was precision in her steps. Not just skill—intention. Poise honed over years, not weeks. She didn't act like a foot soldier or a paid hit. She moved like someone with a reason. A ghost with unfinished business.

Damien watched her frame for several more seconds, then reached down. His fingers found the bottom drawer of the desk, pressed the biometric lock. A soft hiss, a click, and it opened.

Inside was a small, velvet-lined box. Nothing ornate. Just quiet and sacred.

He lifted the lid.

The original Queen of Spades lay inside. Protected. Preserved. Untouched since that night.

The card was worn now—edges softened with time. The top left corner had a slight tear. A mark he remembered causing when he clutched it too tightly the first night Domenico died.

But it was the stain that haunted him. The blood. Still dark. Still there.

His thumb traced it slowly. The weight of it, heavier than it looked.

He sat. Placed the card beside the image frozen on the screen. The new one. Same suit. Same face. But this time, not a remnant. A message.

His jaw locked.

"Someone's trying to finish what they started," he muttered under his breath.

A sharp knock came from the door. One rap. Then silence.

"Come in."

One of his security lieutenants stepped in, standing rigid at the threshold. "No trace yet. But we're working the footage from surrounding blocks."

"Facial recognition?"

"Running now. Encrypted comms detected, but nothing's clean. She's good."

Damien didn't answer. He picked up the old card, weighed it between his fingers, then set it back into the box with careful precision.

"She's not just good," he said quietly. "She's deliberate."

He dismissed the man with a nod. The door shut behind him with a soft click.

Alone again, Damien stood and walked to the bar cabinet. Poured two fingers of Lagavulin. Let it sit. The burn wasn't the point. The ritual was.

He didn't drink it. Just stared into the amber surface like it might tell him something.

"She wants a war," he murmured. "Or maybe justice."

His voice dropped.

"Either way, she's getting fire."

He turned back to the desk. Opened a folder marked with a single word: *Domenico*.

Photos. Police reports. Surveillance stills from that night.

His brother's face, frozen in the final moments of life.

The Queen of Spades on his chest.

The camera footage from hours before the hit. The shadowed figures moving in and out of Syndicate territory.

All the pieces were here. They always had been.

But for years, the trail had been cold. Until tonight.

Damien set his glass down, untouched. Picked up the photo of his brother. Let it sit in his palm.

"You told me never to let emotion cloud the game," he whispered. "But this? This isn't emotion. It's clarity."

His hand clenched, crumpling the edge of the photo just slightly.

"Someone sent that card to mock you. To mock us. Now they want me to find them."

He looked back at the screen.

"Fine," he said. "Game on."

He pressed a button on his phone.

"Get everyone in. Clean team only. No leaks. No hesitation. I want every contact, ally, rival, and ghost combed through until we find her."

"And when we do, sir?"

Damien stared at the screen.

The woman in black leather. Eyes like war.

He smiled, but there was no warmth in it. Only promise.

"Don't kill her," he said. "Not until I've asked her one question."

Pause.

"And not until she answers with blood."

CHAPTER 3

– Caught -

THE ALLEY WAS too clean.

Valentina adjusted the brim of her cap, stepping through the back gate of the derelict building with the ease of a ghost. Her boots were silent. Her breath measured. Her pulse—a steady thrum beneath Kevlar and resolve.

A breeze drifted through the metal framework of the old shipping yard, brushing across rusted beams and cracked concrete. It smelled like oil, steel, and something she couldn't quite name—something wrong.

She scanned the lot. Warehouse C, dead ahead. According to Gia, it was a low-tier Syndicate storage site. No guards on record. No security worth writing home about.

Which made it perfect bait.

Her gloved fingers tightened around the grip of her pistol. One suppressor, one full clip, and a knife strapped beneath her jacket. Not much, but enough.

She'd done more with less.

"Gia, talk to me," she whispered into the comms mic tucked behind her jawline.

The line was static.

Faint. Fuzzy.

Then—gone.

Valentina froze. That wasn't just interference. That was a kill switch.

She crouched beside a crate, eyes narrowing, heart rate jumping just a beat faster. She tapped the mic again. "Gia?"

Silence answered.

Not good.

She reached into her jacket, pulling out a burner phone. No signal. No satellite. The streetlights above flickered once.

Then everything went dark.

Her instincts screamed.

She spun—

Pain.

A flash of white-hot electricity tore through her. Her muscles seized. She hit the ground hard, cheek slamming against concrete.

She tried to move, tried to reach—

Another jolt, sharper this time. Her vision dimmed at the edges.

Voices.

Boots approaching.

Then darkness.

A Room with No Name

When consciousness returned, it was slow.

The light overhead was dim—flickering with that cold, buzzing hum of old fluorescents. The air was metallic, dry, stripped of anything human.

Valentina blinked once. Twice.

Pain bloomed in her shoulders when she tried to move. Her arms were pulled behind her, bound with zip ties tight enough to cut skin. Her ankles—same story.

Panic tried to rise. She shoved it down. Panic was for amateurs.

She catalogued: no visible injuries, just a pulsing ache in her side. Her jacket was gone. Her comms too. Her boots remained. Knife—missing.

Strategic. Not random.

Whoever took her knew exactly what they were doing.

A soft hiss came from the far wall.

A door.

Then footsteps. Measured. Heavy.

She didn't look up right away. Didn't need to.

She could feel him before she saw him.

That presence. The same coiled energy she'd seen in the footage Gia decrypted. That careful coldness, like a predator who knew he never had to rush the kill.

Damien Moreau.

He stepped into the room like he owned gravity. Black shirt, sleeves rolled to the elbows, no tie. Power, stripped bare. His eyes were molten steel—cold and cutting—but something else lingered behind them.

Recognition.

Valentina lifted her chin, spine straightening despite the binds. "If this is your idea of a meet-cute, you're shit at it."

Damien didn't smile. He didn't blink. He just stared.

Then, finally, "You're smaller than I thought."

She snorted. "Sorry to disappoint. Want to untie me and let me make it up to you?"

"No."

He took another step. Slowly. Deliberately. "I like seeing you restrained. It's the first time you're not running."

"You think this ends with me begging?"

"I don't expect you to beg," he said, crouching down in front of her. His voice lowered. "But I do expect you to listen."

She met his gaze, unflinching. "Say whatever you brought me here to say, Moreau. Then go back to whatever brooding villain lair you crawled out of."

Damien reached into his coat pocket.

Pulled something out.

Her card.

The Queen of Spades. Blood-smeared.

Her signature.

He held it between two fingers and slowly, delicately, turned it in the light.

Valentina didn't react. Not visibly.

But inside, her stomach coiled.

"I've seen this card before," he said quietly. "It was on my brother's chest the night he bled out in the snow. Did you know that?"

Her lips parted, but no words came.

He leaned closer. "Did you leave it there then too?"

"I wasn't even in Monaco back then," she said.

"Convenient."

"Truth."

Damien stood. "You torched my facility. You stole my product. You left this."

"Seems you got the message."

His jaw flexed. A muscle ticked beneath his eye. Still calm. Still cold. But she saw it now—the flicker beneath the surface. The man trying not to burn.

"Tell me who you're working for."

"No."

His tone didn't rise. His volume didn't shift. But the temperature in the room dropped.

He circled her now, slow and surgical. "You're not one of the Syndicate's mercs. You're too good. Too careful. That means someone sent you."

"No one sent me."

"You don't act without purpose. You don't strike without reason. So tell me, Russo—"

She flinched.

Damien stopped. "Ah. So that's the nerve."

Her jaw set. "You know who I am."

"I knew the moment I saw the way you moved. You're not just good, you're trained. Russo style. Your father's shadow."

"He's not my anything."

"Still using his last name."

"Still breathing. Want to question that too?"

He walked to the table in the corner of the room. Picked up a file. Opened it. Pages rustled as he flipped through photos.

Surveillance. Of her. Of Gia. Of Ezra.

He tossed the last one in front of her. Gia—blindfolded,

bruised, bound to a chair.

Valentina's heart stopped.

Damien watched her reaction like a scientist observing a flame.

"You're playing a game you don't fully understand," he said. "And the people you care about are the ones who'll pay."

She stared at the photo, then up at him. Her voice was ice. "If you touch her—"

"I haven't. Yet. That depends on you."

Silence stretched between them.

Then, Damien stepped closer. Lowered himself until their eyes met again.

"You torched my family's legacy," he said, voice low, deliberate. "Now I own yours."

She didn't flinch. Didn't look away. But in that moment, she knew this wasn't the end of something.

It was the beginning.

CHAPTER 4

- Predator's Game -

THE ROOM HAD changed, not physically. Not in its square-foot dimensions or the faint buzz of flickering overhead lights. But in atmosphere, it felt as if the air had thickened.

Damien didn't rush.

He walked in, perfectly composed, as though he were entering a meeting room and not the chamber of someone who'd burned down a part of his empire. He carried no weapon. No clipboard. No interrogator's mask.

He didn't need one.

Power wasn't in what you showed—it was in what you withheld.

Valentina sat in the metal chair where he'd left her, arms still bound behind her, ankles crossed and zip-tied, but her posture had changed. She no longer looked like a cornered wolf. Now, she looked like she was waiting to be amused.

"Come to trade war stories?" she asked.

Damien said nothing for a long moment. Just pulled out the other chair, sat down across from her, and leveled a gaze that could disassemble most men.

"You're quick with words," he said. "That's the first mask to go when people start breaking."

"I don't break."

"No?"

She leaned forward, just a little. "You've got the voice of a man who thinks pain is a currency. I've survived men like you before. You don't scare me."

Damien tilted his head slightly. "Good. Fear clouds judgment. I want clarity when I give you a choice."

Her eyes narrowed, a flicker of something passing across her features.

"I don't recall asking for a choice."

"You didn't."

Silence again. Long and sharp.

Then:

"Tell me why you targeted that facility," he said.

She shrugged. "Didn't like the paint job."

Damien gave a quiet smile that didn't reach his eyes. "You're not a vigilante. You're methodical. Tactical. Your heist was clean, your escape cleaner. That wasn't rebellion. That was precision."

"And yet," she said coolly, "I'm sitting here zip-tied to a chair. So, how precise could I be?"

"You were good," he admitted. "But not flawless. You underestimated the Syndicate. Or maybe… you underestimated me."

He watched her carefully. The edge of a muscle twitched in her jaw, but she said nothing.

"Someone trained you," he continued. "And trained you well. But training isn't instinct. It doesn't prepare you for the moment when your people bleed."

Her gaze flickered.

Barely. But enough.

Damien leaned forward, forearms resting on his thighs, closing the distance between them.

"This is your only negotiation window, Valentina. After today, I stop asking. You're going to work for me."

That drew a laugh from her—dark, bitter. "You really are delusional."

"Perhaps."

"But I'm not one of your dogs. I don't fetch. I don't beg."

"I didn't say anything about begging."

He let the silence hang again. Controlled. Unhurried. Then he pulled something from the inner pocket of his jacket and placed it on the table between them.

A sleek black folder.

She didn't look at it.

He opened it slowly, revealing surveillance photos—her crew. Ezra, walking out of a bar. Gia, boarding a tram. Another shot: their safehouse door cracked open.

Valentina's body went rigid.

"I know where they are," Damien said, voice quiet. "I know how they move. And I know how to make them disappear without a trace."

"You touch them, and I swear to God—"

"You're not in a position to swear anything."

He stood, walked slowly toward the far end of the room. "You can lie to me. You can even hate me. But what you can't do… is ignore what happens when loyalty is used against you."

He turned and faced her again. "Infiltrate the Russo empire.

Report everything. That's your trade. In return, your team walks free. Untouched."

Valentina's eyes sharpened. "You want me to betray my family."

"No," he said. "I want you to cut it open from the inside. I want names, supply routes, financial flows. You burned one building. I want you to bring down the house."

"And if I say no?"

Damien's jaw tightened.

"Then I stop being civil."

The Devil's Offer

Damien leaned back in his chair, the leather creaking beneath him as he studied her like a puzzle he was halfway through solving.

He hadn't touched her—hadn't needed to. Power didn't always come from contact; sometimes, it lived in silence. In the way he controlled the air between them.

Valentina sat upright, her posture defiant despite the cuffs bruising her wrists. Her mouth was cut, dried blood flaking at the edge. Her eye was beginning to swell, a souvenir from the struggle during her capture.

Yet there was no fear in her expression—only fire. Pure, uncut rage.

"You've been busy," Damien said, voice calm but laced with quiet contempt.

"The facility. The blaze. That little calling card of yours." He tapped his fingers on the table slowly, each tap a beat of warning. "Very theatrical."

Valentina arched a brow. "Did you enjoy the show? I made sure the finale had a bang."

He didn't smile.

"You cost me twenty-three million in product. Three months of covert supply chain logistics. And a man's life."

Her eyes narrowed. "You kill men like I change boots."

"Not that man," he said, the words clipped. "He was mine."

The air seemed to shift. Her breath caught—not from fear, but from recognition. This wasn't about business. This was personal. That changed everything.

He stood, walked slowly to the shelf behind him, and pulled down a sleek black tablet. With a swipe of his thumb, the screen came to life. He set it down in front of her, tilting it just enough for her to see.

The screen was blank for a moment. Then: footage.

Security cam feed. Grainy, timestamped. A room, sterile and bare. In the center—Gia.

Her hair was matted, blood on her temple. Her lips were cracked, her breathing shallow. She was bound to a metal chair, her hands trembling in her lap. A man moved across the frame—faceless, back to the camera—but he shoved her roughly, and she whimpered.

Valentina's body went rigid. Her knuckles turned white against the steel cuffs. For a moment, her mouth parted as if to speak, but no words came. Just a sound—a breath, choked and wounded.

Damien watched her. Not with pleasure, but with purpose.

"You've built a nice little rebellion," he said softly. "But rebellions get people killed. Innocent ones. Loyal ones."

Her jaw clenched, a muscle twitching near her temple. She forced her gaze away from the screen, her voice a low rasp.

"What do you want?"

He leaned in. The space between them crackled.

"I want you to go home, Valentina. I want you to kiss your father on both cheeks and pretend you're the prodigal daughter. I want you to play your part—smile at his men, listen at the doors, dance with devils—and tell me everything."

She shook her head, once, sharply. "I'll die before I give you anything."

He tilted his head. "That's not what I asked."

Silence stretched, oppressive and long. Her eyes flicked back to the screen. Gia was still breathing, but just barely. And for the first time, her armor cracked. Her spine slumped half an inch. Her breath trembled.

Damien saw it—and didn't push. He stood, locked the tablet again, and returned to his seat.

"The choice is yours," he said. "But every hour you hesitate, she bleeds a little more."

Valentina's lips parted. Her voice was hoarse.

"You son of a bitch."

He didn't deny it.

After Damien left the room, the silence swallowed her whole.

The door's click echoed like a gunshot. For a few seconds, she didn't move. Her body was still, eyes trained on the spot where the screen had gone black.

The image of Gia, tied and helpless, branded itself onto the backs of her eyelids like a scar that wouldn't heal.

She exhaled slowly, and with that breath came the first tremor. Not from fear—but from restraint. Every instinct screamed for violence, but she was trapped.

Not just by the cuffs or the walls. Trapped by the cost of loyalty.

"Fuck," she whispered.

The room was cold, lit only by a bulb hanging from the ceiling like a noose. The walls were matte steel, silent witnesses to the moment her world began to fracture.

She slumped forward, resting her head against the edge of the table.

Gia had saved her once. Dragged her bleeding out of an alley in Naples when Valentina was seventeen and half-dead from a Russo beating.

Gia had hacked the cameras, forged the ID, and burned a trail so clean even the Devil couldn't follow it. And now she was paying the price for Valentina's war.

Her pride didn't matter anymore. Her pain didn't matter. All that mattered was not letting Gia become collateral damage.

Valentina lifted her head. Her face was pale, but her eyes burned with a new kind of fire—not fury, not revenge. Resolve.

"Alright," she muttered into the silence. "You win."

Not forever. Not completely. But for now.

She knew what this game was. She knew what Damien Moreau was.

And she was going to play it better than he ever expected.

Because when the Queen of Spades folds—it's only to reshuffle the deck.

CHAPTER 5

– THE CRACK –

SHE SAID IT through clenched teeth. "Fine. I'll do it."

The words were acid on her tongue—burning with every syllable, each one a nail in her pride. She didn't look at him when she spoke. She couldn't.

Because if she did—if she met those eyes, colder than any steel she'd ever handled—she might have thrown the table across the room instead.

Damien didn't react. No smirk. No slow, self-satisfied lean back in his chair. He only studied her with the same impenetrable calm he wore like armor, as if her reluctant submission were inevitable. Expected.

"I'll have the first set of instructions to you within the hour," he said quietly. "You'll need to make contact with your father by the end of the week. Your story has already been fabricated. You were injured. Out of touch. Lost. But now you're back. Changed."

Valentina said nothing.

He paused. "You'll be welcomed, but not trusted. Use that. Suspicion opens more doors than blind faith."

Still, she didn't answer.

"Gia's alive," he added. "For now. Prove you're worth the risk I'm taking, and she stays that way."

Valentina's hand twitched in her lap.

He didn't see it—but she felt the phantom weight of her gun, the twitch of instinct that told her where the trigger would be, how fast she could raise it.

But there was no gun here. No power. Only this room. Only him. And the deal she had just made with the devil.

Damien stood. His footsteps were silent against the concrete floor as he moved toward the door.

"You'll be transferred to a safe house tonight," he said, pausing with his hand on the frame. "Eat. Rest. You'll need both."

Then he was gone.

And she was left behind. With silence. With herself.

Guilt Is a Blade

The room emptied of his presence, but the echo of him remained—like smoke in her lungs. She leaned forward slowly, her elbows pressing into her thighs, her fingers curled into fists so tight her knuckles blanched. Her heart beat a war drum in her chest, but her face remained still. Cold.

Gia.

It always came back to Gia.

The first time she met her, they were fifteen. A heist gone sideways. Valentina bleeding in a stairwell, her ankle twisted, a dozen Syndicate dogs combing the streets. Gia had found her by accident. Didn't ask questions. Just pulled her out, hacking security cams and rewriting access logs as they moved. She didn't owe her a damn thing.

But she saved her.

And from that moment on, Gia became family. Real family—the kind you didn't inherit by blood or name but by the scars you were willing to earn for each other.

Valentina squeezed her eyes shut. In the darkness, she saw the girl she remembered: short hair dyed a different color every month, calloused fingers typing at lightning speed, a laugh that sounded like rebellion. And now—tied to a chair, crying, bruised.

That image hadn't left her since Damien played the video.

It haunted her. Clawed at her ribs. Wrapped around her spine like barbed wire and refused to let go.

He was playing her. She knew that. Gia was leverage. A chess piece. But that didn't make it any less real. Gia was hurting. And Valentina had the key to stop it.

She would get her back.

And then she'd make Damien Moreau bleed for ever thinking he could hold the leash.

But for now… she would play along. For now, she would let him believe he'd won.

The worst part was knowing he hadn't lost.

Quiet Fury

Night came slowly, seeping through the small window like oil. Valentina hadn't moved in hours. She'd eaten what they brought her—barely—but hadn't spoken since Damien left. The walls didn't talk back anyway. They just absorbed her anger.

Her transfer happened quietly. Two guards she didn't know. No Syndicate insignias. Clean suits. Blank faces. They moved like ghosts and treated her like a package—not a person.

The safe house was nondescript. Brick. Remote. Inside, it

smelled of bleach and stale air. A bedroom. A bathroom. No weapons. One window, sealed. A phone, already preloaded with encrypted apps.

When they left her alone, she sat on the edge of the bed, still as death.

This wasn't submission.

This was strategy.

Valentina pulled off her boots slowly, methodically, as if each movement was its own kind of vow. She laid back, stared at the ceiling, and let the silence press against her skin.

Damien thought he had her.

But he didn't know her—not really. Not the parts carved from grief and vengeance. Not the pieces she kept hidden even from herself. He thought she'd crack.

He didn't understand that this *was* her cracked.

That beneath this still surface was a fire waiting to consume everything in its path.

She turned her head to the side. The faint hum of electricity buzzed in the walls. The light above her flickered once and held.

She whispered into the dark, more to herself than anyone else.

"You just made the biggest mistake of your life."

And when she finally closed her eyes, sleep didn't come easy.

Because she was already planning how to end him.

CHAPTER 6

- Vow of Fire -

VALENTINA STOOD IN THE sterile confines of a room that smelled like antiseptic and cold calculation. Overhead, a single bulb buzzed faintly, its pale light casting a shadow beneath her eyes.

Her wrists bore faint, bruised reminders of her earlier restraints, but she held her posture like a queen who'd never been on her knees.

Valentina Russo was no longer the furious, caged woman spitting threats through clenched teeth.

She had recalibrated.

Damien had entered moments before. No words. Just a glance —measured, guarded. Between them, a silence that didn't need breaking. It pulsed like a live wire, heavy with things unsaid.

He approached without hesitation, extending a small burner phone toward her. She didn't reach for it at first. Instead, her eyes found his—cold meeting colder.

It was a battle of stillness. His jaw ticked once, and that was all she needed.

She took the phone.

Their fingers didn't brush. Their gazes didn't shift. It was a transaction, but under its surface churned something deeper—volatile, electric.

Still, neither of them blinked.

Then he turned and walked out.

She didn't follow.

Not yet.

Instead, she stood there for a breath longer, letting the silence settle around her like armor. She opened the phone, found only a single contact number marked with a fire emoji. No name. Just symbolism. Subtle, and stupidly poetic.

Typical of him.

She pocketed the device and exhaled slowly, deliberately, as if shedding the skin of the girl who had screamed behind duct tape and fury.

That girl was gone.

In her place stood something sharper.

Something forged.

The Car Ride to Hell

The car smelled like leather and menace. Blacked-out windows, bulletproof shell, and the thick silence of secrets. The driver—silent and unrecognizable—never turned around or acknowledged her presence.

That was part of the protocol, part of Damien's design.

She didn't care.

She stared out the window as the city passed in fractured shadows. Neon lights cut through fog like blades. The wet streets reflected everything upside down—appropriate, considering her life had just been flipped inside out.

She memorized the route.

She always did.

But it wasn't the streets that consumed her.

It was the war unraveling in her head.

Gia...

The name was a knife. Each memory of her friend—arms scabbed from a broken childhood, laughter that always bordered on hysteria, the way she always fixed what was broken—tightened the noose around Valentina's ribcage.

Gia had saved her once. Pulled her from a hellish overdose in a Naples alley when she was nineteen and running from her father's empire. That night, she'd sworn to return the favor.

And now... she would.

The mission Damien proposed was madness. She knew it. He knew it. The Russo estate wasn't just a house—it was a trap masquerading as family.

Cameras in the chandeliers. Guns in the wine racks. Loyalty bought in blood.

Going back was a suicide note written in lipstick and pride.

But Gia was worth it.

So was the reckoning she'd been preparing for years.

In the reflection of the window, she studied herself. The cleaned-up exterior. The subtle bruising along her cheekbone, camouflaged under concealer. Her hair slicked back into a braid like a soldier reporting for war.

"I'll play your game, Damien," she thought, her voice a whisper in her skull. "But I'll make the board mine."

She let her head fall back against the seat. Closed her eyes. Let her pulse sync with the rhythm of the tires rolling over cracked asphalt. She imagined the moment her father would see her. What would flicker in his eyes first—relief? Suspicion? Rage?

It didn't matter.

She would weaponize all of it.

The Return to the Cage

The car turned down the long, winding drive flanked by whispering cypress trees that swayed like silent sentinels. The wind caught in their branches, and for a moment, it sounded like a thousand murmurs chasing her from behind—ghosts of the past, voices of things buried but not dead.

Valentina sat still, hands folded in her lap like a sculpture carved from defiance and dread.

As the mansion rose into view, she felt her chest tighten—not with fear, but with memory. The kind that settled behind the ribs like old shrapnel. She hadn't seen this place in two years, but it hadn't changed.

Not a crack in the facade, not a chip in the marble columns. Time didn't erode what was protected by fear and fortified by blood.

The iron gates loomed, familiar and towering, etched with the Russo crest—two lions flanking a sword wrapped in laurel. Victory or death. That was the family motto, though no one ever said it out loud. They didn't need to. It was embedded in their bones.

The driver slowed as the intercom buzzed. A pause. Then a crisp voice: "Authorization?"

"Valentina Russo," she said clearly, her voice cold and deliberate.

Another pause. She could almost hear the hesitation on the other end.

Then the gates groaned open, metal against metal, and the car rolled forward with a reverent quiet.

She didn't look at the house. Not yet.

Instead, she turned her head and watched the gates close behind her, slow and final, until they sealed with a soft click that sounded far too much like a lock engaging.

No escape now.

Not without blood.

The gravel under the tires shifted as the car circled the grand fountain at the estate's center. It was a grotesque thing—stone cherubs vomiting water dyed deep red to resemble wine.

Her father's idea of opulence. Or a warning. Maybe both.

She stepped out of the car before the driver could come around. She didn't want help. Didn't want ceremony.

Her boots met the ground with a sharp crunch, and she stood tall, letting the chill of the coastal wind rush into her lungs.

It smelled of citrus and salt, and beneath that, the faint sting of bleach and gun oil. The perfume of the Russo estate.

Lights bathed the house in golden glow, but no warmth came from them. Every window gleamed like a watchful eye. The front doors, carved from centuries-old walnut, were shut tight, two guards standing on either side with rifles slung over their chests and expressions carved from stone.

Neither spoke. Neither moved. But both looked at her.

She met their stares, unflinching.

The doors opened.

And there he was.

Sergio Russo.

Her father.

He stood in the entryway like a king expecting tribute. His silver hair was perfectly combed, his black suit crisp, his hands behind his back. Only his eyes moved—piercing, calculating, betraying no emotion.

For a long moment, they simply looked at each other. No embrace. No welcome.

Just the old, well-worn silence of power meeting rebellion.

"You're late," he said.

Valentina offered a smile. Not warm. Not kind. A blade with a curve.

"Traffic," she said.

He studied her, but made no move toward affection. It was all part of the performance. Power was never supposed to bend first.

Still, something flickered in his expression. A twitch in the corner of his mouth. The faintest crease between his brows. Was it surprise? Relief? Suspicion?

She didn't care.

She walked past him without permission.

The foyer was exactly as she remembered—high ceilings, oil paintings of dead men who'd once ruled over cities, marble floors so polished they looked like sheets of ice. The chandelier above glittered like a crown suspended by a single string.

She hated every inch of it.

Memories trailed her steps like shadows—nights spent hiding under staircases during gunfire, learning to lie with a smile at thirteen, watching her mother weep in silence with a glass of vermouth trembling in her hand.

Home.

Her mother's portrait still hung above the fireplace, immortalized in oil and illusion.

The woman in the painting had elegance, beauty, and a softness that Valentina barely remembered. In truth, her mother had been a ghost long before she died. Consumed by the very empire her husband built.

Valentina stopped for a heartbeat too long, looking up at the painting. A pulse of grief bloomed and vanished, as quick as a blink.

Then she moved on.

Through the corridor, the scent of polished wood and money seeped into her bones. The staff she passed gave polite nods, eyes flicking down, trained not to stare. She could see it in them, though.

The curiosity. The wariness. Like they were seeing a revenant returned from the dead.

She reached her old bedroom and stepped inside.

It hadn't changed.

Her books still lined the shelves, alphabetized as she'd left them. The record player in the corner still bore the dust of disuse. Her bed—queen-sized, neatly made, untouched—felt like a stage prop.

This room was a museum exhibit of a life she no longer claimed.

She shut the door and locked it.

Then she leaned her back against it and exhaled. Slowly. Shakily.

Her hand went to her wrist, fingers brushing the skin where the restraints had bruised her. She didn't wince. Not anymore. Pain had become part of the language she spoke fluently.

She walked to the mirror and stared at herself.

The girl who'd once dreamed of escape, of building her own life away from the Russo name, was long gone.

In her place stood a soldier.

A spy.

A timebomb ticking quietly behind the lines.

She opened the drawer beside her bed. Slid her fingers along the wood until they found the old switchblade tucked behind a stack of journals. She palmed it with practiced ease and smiled. Some things, at least, still belonged to her.

As the house settled around her, the creaks and whispers of the walls began to stir like old bones waking from slumber. Every sound had meaning here. Every silence was deliberate.

She knew how to listen.

Valentina crossed to the window, pulled the curtain back an inch, and stared out at the night.

The gates had closed behind her.

But she hadn't come back to stay.

She'd come back to burn it down.

CHAPTER 7

- Gilded Cage -

THE IRON GATES creaked open like the jaws of something ancient and patient. Valentina sat in the backseat, spine straight, fingers curled tightly in her lap.

As the car rolled down the gravel path that led to the Russo estate, she stared at the towering stone façade, its high arches and wrought-iron balconies unchanged. Except now, everything seemed smaller.

Or maybe she had simply grown sharper. Harder.

The house wasn't just a home—it was a monument to control. Polished marble. Cold halls. A palace built on silence and blood.

She stepped out, boots crunching on gravel, chin high despite the weight dragging in her chest.

A breeze carried the scent of the vineyards and the faintest trace of rosewater—her mother's perfume still lived in the bones of this place.

Marco Russo stood on the front steps, flanked by two men in tailored suits. His smile spread easily, but it stopped short of his eyes.

"The prodigal daughter returns," he said, arms open.

Valentina didn't embrace him. She offered a nod, just enough for the eyes watching from the shadows. "Father."

Behind Marco, Enzo lingered like a vulture in human skin. His dark eyes narrowed slightly, reading her as if she were a cipher to crack. He didn't speak, but his posture did. He was ready for a lie. He expected it.

Inside, nothing had changed. The grand chandelier above the foyer glittered like a thousand tiny knives. Portraits of her ancestors stared down from the walls, their painted gazes smug and judgmental.

A butler took her coat, and still, the air remained cold.

"News travels fast," Marco said, guiding her toward the drawing room.

"You being in New York. The Syndicate raid. Some are already whispering your name."

"I'm just reconnecting with my blood," she said smoothly. "Is that such a crime?"

Marco laughed, the sound brittle. "We're all criminals, cara. The trick is keeping your sins profitable."

She didn't smile.

Memory Is A Minefield

The door creaked open like a sigh from the past.

Valentina stepped inside her childhood bedroom, and for a moment—just one, fleeting moment—she forgot she was on a mission. The scent hit her first. Faded jasmine, dust, and the faint metallic tang of old perfume bottles clinging to the vanity.

The air was heavy with time, each breath catching somewhere between nostalgia and suffocation.

Everything was still here. Unmoved. Untouched.

A silk scarf draped over the chair, the color dulled from sunlight. A row of porcelain dolls gathering dust on a high shelf.

Her childhood sketchbook half-open on the desk, filled with softer things from a time when her world had not yet sharpened into daggers.

The rug beneath her boots was the same one she used to lie on, staring up at the ceiling, wondering what freedom might feel like.

The room was a shrine. Not to her—but to the version of her Marco had wanted to preserve. A daughter who stayed obedient.

A daughter who never left. A daughter who never learned how to burn.

She moved toward the dresser, her fingers ghosting across the top. A photograph rested in a silver frame—her, at sixteen, standing between Marco and her mother. The smile on her lips was too small. Her mother's was warm, almost painfully so.

Marco's hand gripped her shoulder with a kind of possessive pride.

She stared at it now, tilting it toward the light, seeing for the first time the bruising truth behind the angle of his fingers.

She set it down carefully. Then opened the drawer.

Inside, neatly folded, were her old journals. Pages of poetry and plans and quiet rebellion. She flipped through one, her handwriting looping and unsure, the words naive and full of longing. One line caught her eye:

"If I leave, do I lose the right to come home?"

She closed it. No. This was not home. Not anymore.

A soft knock on the door startled her.

A maid entered—young, unfamiliar, eyes lowered with professional deference. She carried fresh linens and a timid smile.

"Miss Russo," the girl said, and for a second Valentina flinched at the name. "Your room has been prepared as requested."

"I didn't request anything."

The maid paused, clearly unsure. "Your father... asked that everything be made comfortable for your return."

Valentina nodded once. "Thank you. That will be all."

When the girl left, closing the door with a whisper, Valentina returned to her feet. She needed to move. She needed to *think*.

Because comfort wasn't kindness. Not here. Comfort was control.

She slipped from her boots, tied her hair back, and began to walk the halls. Quiet. Careful. Familiar.

Her body remembered the way like muscle memory—where to step to avoid creaking wood, which doors led to hidden rooms, which corners had blind spots from the security cameras. But things had changed. The walls had new eyes.

Cameras embedded in the crown molding. Reinforced doors with digital keypads where simple locks once stood. The guards had changed too—more uniformed men, fewer smiles.

And they all wore the same expression: watchfulness dressed as respect.

She passed through the west hallway and paused before a door that used to lead to her mother's art studio. It was locked now.

Heavy and unwelcoming. The smell of paint and turpentine had long faded, replaced by sterile silence.

Her fingers brushed the wall beside it, pausing on a faint dent in the plaster. Oval-shaped. A bruise that never healed.

She didn't cry. She couldn't afford to.

Downstairs, she slipped into the drawing room, lingering in the shadowed archway.

Marco was on the phone, speaking in low, clipped Italian.

"They want confirmation before the week ends. Yes, the engagement will be announced at the gala. She doesn't need to know until the deal is done."

Valentina's chest tightened. The words weren't entirely clear, but the implication was. Her father hadn't brought her home for love. He'd brought her back for leverage.

Pawn, not prodigal.

She backed away before the call ended, retracing her steps in reverse. She filed away the information. Every hallway, every whisper, every coded phrase would feed into the map she was building in her head.

The only way to win was to know the ground better than the enemy.

And in this house, everyone was the enemy.

Even blood.

Back in her room, she peeled off her coat and laid it over the chair. Her reflection caught in the vanity mirror—tired, pale, but with something simmering just below the surface. Not fear. Not anymore.

Resolve.

There was no time for softness. Not even for grief.

Not even for memories that clung like cobwebs in her chest.

She looked around the room again and knew—truly knew—this place had never been hers. Not in any meaningful way. It had been a cage designed to look like safety. A velvet prison.

But now?

Now it was her battlefield.

And she intended to bleed it dry.

Blood In The Walls

The Russo estate didn't creak. It groaned.

Late at night, after the staff had retreated into their quarters and the guards rotated to their midnight posts, Valentina walked the marble halls barefoot. Silence should have been comforting, but in this house, it echoed. Every sound had weight.

Every breath, a ripple. The very walls seemed to hold memories like stains soaked into stone.

She knew these halls better than anyone. Or at least she used to.

Now, every turn felt slightly off. As if the house itself had been restructured in her absence—not physically, but spiritually. It no longer welcomed her. It studied her. Tracked her with the gaze of old ghosts.

She paused by the grand staircase. A patch of floor there, slightly paler than the rest. She remembered the day it was scrubbed raw. She had been thirteen. A servant had spilled wine during dinner—clumsy, trembling—and Marco had responded with the kind of discipline that required silence.

The next morning, Valentina found blood smudged beneath the table leg. Her mother had sent the staff home early that day. Told Valentina not to ask questions.

But she had always known.

This house had always fed on fear. She just hadn't known how deeply.

Now, older, wiser, carved into steel, she could see it clearly. The walls were dressed in opulence—gold-leaf frames, priceless paintings, velvet-trimmed wallpaper—but beneath that glittered decay.

The chandeliers sparkled, but the air beneath them was thick with secrets.

She descended the stairs, the cold stone biting at her skin, and moved toward the east wing. The oldest part of the estate. Forgotten by design.

The doors here had swollen from disuse, and the floorboards sighed beneath her weight.

Her hand ran along the carved rail of the corridor as she walked, fingertips grazing decades of varnished deceit.

She paused at a door.

It used to be her grandfather's study. A room Marco never entered.

She turned the handle slowly. It resisted, then gave way with a soft click.

Inside, dust blanketed every surface. Shafts of moonlight spilled through the high windows, cutting the dark like silver blades. The room smelled like old leather, whiskey, and secrets—preserved like a tomb.

Books lined the walls, many with pages yellowed and curling.

A chessboard sat mid-game by the fireplace. The white queen missing.

Her breath caught in her throat as she stepped deeper into the room. Every inch of this space whispered of another era—another hierarchy of violence.

Her grandfather had ruled the family before Marco. Harsher, some said. But fair in ways Marco never was. He believed in codes.

In consequences. Marco believed only in control.

She walked to the desk. Thick, heavy, carved from oak. She pulled open a drawer.

Inside, nestled beneath old correspondence and yellowed

maps, was a single item that didn't belong.

A Queen of Spades card.

Crisp. Clean. New.

She stared at it, throat tightening.

Not hers. Not her message. Someone had been here before her.

Or someone was leaving breadcrumbs.

She picked it up and flipped it over. A single word in red ink.

"Traitor."

A sound behind her made her whirl around, heart racing—but the hallway remained empty.

She tucked the card into her pocket and backed out of the room, pulse pounding. Every step away felt heavier than the last, like the house was trying to keep her there.

Back in the safety of her bedroom—if it could be called that—she locked the door behind her and pressed her back against it.

Someone knew.

Someone inside the house was playing their own game. One she hadn't seen coming.

She moved to the window and looked out over the gardens, now overgrown and unkempt. Even the roses had thorns longer than she remembered.

Gia. Ezra. Her crew. She couldn't protect them if she was blind to the players in this house.

And Damien... Damien had said nothing about this.

Was it a warning? A taunt? A test?

Or something worse?

Her fingers traced the card in her pocket. The Queen of Spades had always been her mark. Her threat. Her signature. But now it had turned on her. Used against her. Turned into a curse.

She leaned against the glass, fogging it with her breath. The estate loomed behind her like a fortress made of ghosts.

Valentina didn't feel like a daughter returned anymore.

She felt like a soldier in enemy uniform.

And the blood in these walls?

It wasn't dried. It was waiting.

CHAPTER 8

- Eyes in the Walls -

VALENTINA MOVED LIKE a phantom through the bowels of the Russo estate. The grand halls above—bathed in opulence, gold trim, and polite deception—were a stark contrast to the skeletal underbelly beneath. Stone walls bled dampness.

Wine cellars gave way to forgotten tunnels and hollowed-out corridors built long before her birth. The Russo empire was not just built on power. It was built on secrets.

She trailed her fingers along the rough walls, remembering childhood whispers—rumors of escape tunnels, of hidden passageways used during wartime and blood feuds. Now, they were the estate's silent lungs.

She found a disused security hub tucked behind a false wall in the cellar.

Dust covered half the monitors, but the others? Live feeds of the estate—bedrooms, gates, gardens. Every move was watched. Every breath recorded.

She made mental notes. Guard rotations. Surveillance blind spots. Passcodes muttered between underbosses who didn't realize she was listening.

She was good at fading into spaces. At becoming the silence itself.

But silence didn't last long.

She turned a corner too fast. Enzo stood there—sharp-suited, snake-eyed, smiling like the devil on a good day.

"You think we don't see the games you play?" he murmured, stepping closer until the scent of his cologne was all she could breathe.

"Careful, bambina. You're not untouchable."

She didn't flinch. Not outwardly. But inside? The familiar ice climbed her spine.

"And you're not as clever as you think, Enzo," she said, her voice calm, cold, surgical.

"Keep testing me. Let's see who draws blood first."

He held her gaze for one beat too long, then smiled and stepped aside. She walked past him with steel in her spine, but her pulse didn't slow until she was out of sight.

Back in her old room, she closed the door and locked it. Her mother's jewelry box still sat untouched on the vanity—ivory and brass, cracked at the hinges.

She opened it and slipped the burner phone beneath the satin lining.

With the curtains drawn and the lights dimmed, she began her ritual.

She fed Damien everything.

Encrypted files from Marco's study. Shipment dates. Passwords scribbled on the back of a menu. A camera layout she'd mapped from memory. Every piece she collected, she passed like a ghost in the machine.

That night, she took the long path to the vineyard chapel—long since abandoned, but not forgotten. She knew the way by heart. Her boots crunched gravel. Her breath fogged in the cool night air.

Moonlight cut across the chapel floor through shattered stained glass, painting red and blue on ancient stone.

Behind the altar, tucked beneath loose floorboards, she found a folded note. Small. Precise. His handwriting.

"Good girl."

Two words. No signature. No instructions.

It made her fists clench. Her pulse spike. Fury flared—but it wasn't clean. It came tangled with something darker. Something hotter.

She hated the part of her that liked it. The part that responded to his praise like oxygen to flame.

She burned the note before leaving. But the words were already carved beneath her skin.

Through A Predator's Lens

High in the hills, where the vineyard sloped into shadow and the estate was no more than a quiet breath in the valley below, Damien adjusted the scope of the rifle without urgency.

He lay prone on a nest of rock and gravel, the wind curling around his coat like a whisper of warning. The night was clear—too clear.

The kind of clarity that stripped the world bare and made liars out of men who preferred fog to truth.

Through the scope, he could see her.

Valentina Russo moved like a woman born of war—measured, unsentimental, with a kind of grace honed not in ballroom halls but in back alleys and boardrooms soaked in blood.

She wore her power subtly, like perfume—something that lingered after she passed, that clung to the air like smoke.

She crossed the chapel threshold, her silhouette etched

in moonlight. The abandoned structure swallowed her, stone arches framing her figure like a cathedral meant for saints and sinners alike.

She paused—just briefly—beneath the arch, tilting her head as if listening to the ghosts within.

Or perhaps to him. She didn't know he was there, but some part of her always moved like she did.

Damien adjusted the focus slightly. Not to see her more clearly—he already knew every contour of her. He watched her as a man might watch a storm on the horizon: with reverence, calculation, and the distant ache of inevitability.

She knelt by the altar. He could just make out the flick of her wrist, the slide of floorboards, the slow retrieval of the message he had left behind.

good girl.

The phrase had been intentional. Not cruel—never that—but strategic. Words, he'd learned, were more potent than bullets. And that one? It had lodged itself like a hook behind her ribs. He'd seen it in her body when she read it—how her spine had straightened, how her fingers had curled into fists before she burned the note with a fury she didn't want him to see.

She hated being touched without consent. Even with words.

Especially with praise.

But Damien didn't touch recklessly. He studied. Calculated. He saw her not as a puzzle to be solved, but as a weapon being forged.

She was blade and handle both, and right now, she hadn't decided which way to cut.

A slow smile ghosted across his lips as she exited the chapel, her features briefly illuminated by fractured moonlight spilling through the ruined stained glass.

Crimson and violet slid across her face, making her look less like a spy and more like a specter of vengeance.

He didn't move.

Didn't breathe.

Just watched.

Because this—this was where the war truly lived. Not in gunfights or empires burning. But in quiet moments like this, where the lines between predator and protector blurred.

She had no idea how many times he'd watched her. Protected her from shadows she never knew reached for her. Killed for her before she ever knew his name. Not out of devotion.

Not yet. But something older. Something hungrier. A question he hadn't yet answered:

was she the enemy he had to destroy—or the one who would destroy him?

He traced the sightline back to her eyes as she paused by the old garden wall, her fingers brushing the carved stone roses there. He knew those roses. Had bled on them once.

He exhaled, slow and soundless.

There was something terrifying in her now. Not the kind of fear that made men run.

The kind that made them stay. The kind that promised not death—but transformation.

Through the scope, Damien's voice was a whisper meant for no one but her.

"Keep playing, queen. I've got your back."

He pulled away from the rifle, the night air cool against his skin. Then, with all the quiet elegance of a ghost, he disappeared into the trees, leaving only breathless stillness behind.

But he would return. Always.

Because the game had begun.

And she was already the most dangerous piece on the board.

CHAPTER 9

- Heat of the Chase -

THE NIGHT WAS thick with heat and fog, the kind that clung to skin and made silence feel louder.

Valentina crouched behind rusted cargo crates, the stench of motor oil and damp earth filling her lungs. The port was abandoned—or so it should have been. Instead, voices crackled in the distance. Syndicate men. Heavily armed. Too many.

She swore under her breath.

What should have been a clean intel drop had spiraled into chaos. A last-minute change in the meeting point. An extra shipment not mentioned in the logistics logs.

A guard rotation out of rhythm. She could feel the trap tightening, every breath laced with the metallic taste of risk.

The burner phone in her pocket vibrated once.

Abort. They're onto you.

Damien's message.

Her pulse stuttered. She slipped the phone back into her jacket and made a sharp turn down a shadowed service alley, bootsteps muffled by grit.

Her disguise—a simple black outfit, hat pulled low—wasn't enough now. The guards were on alert, rifles drawn, searching.

And then—

A voice. "Hey! You there!"

She bolted.

The world narrowed into gunmetal and breath. Her feet hit concrete, sharp and quick, weaving between crates and stacks of smuggled goods.

A shot rang out, sparks flying as a bullet struck metal just inches from her shoulder.

Someone grabbed her arm. She twisted, elbowing him hard. But another man lunged from behind, stronger.

He slammed her against a wall. She struggled. His fingers wrapped around her throat.

And then—he dropped.

A spray of blood painted the wall behind him.

Valentina spun. Atop a shipping container, in the darkness, a single red glint flashed. A scope.

Damien.

A breath left her. Not relief. Not safety. Just awareness.

He didn't call out. He didn't wave. He disappeared into the night.

But she knew.

He was watching.

Burned Edges

The alley behind the port was dark, lit only by the flicker of a busted neon sign and the amber glow of cigarette butts crushed into the pavement.

Valentina leaned against the wall, trying to steady her breathing. Her lip was split, blood dripping onto her collar. Her heart thudded like a war drum.

And then he was there.

Damien moved like a shadow peeled from the wall. Controlled. Silent. Drenched in leather and purpose. His eyes scanned her from head to toe, flickering over the torn sleeve, the grazed cheekbone, the blood.

"You were supposed to wait for confirmation," he said, voice low, hard.

She shoved off the wall. "You're welcome for the tip."

He stepped forward. "You almost died."

"So did your men."

"That was the backup plan. You weren't."

Valentina barked a sharp laugh. "You think I need protecting?"

He didn't answer. Just closed the space between them in one step.

She didn't back away.

The tension crackled like static before a storm, fierce and magnetic.

He slammed a hand against the wall beside her head. Not touching. Not yet. But too close.

"I told you to be careful."

"And I told you not to tell me what to do."

It wasn't a scream. It wasn't a whisper. It was a growl in the dark.

His hand came to her jaw—not soft, not cruel. Just command, pure and sharp. Her breath hitched. His thumb brushed the edge of her mouth, smearing blood she hadn't noticed.

"You bleed for this war," he murmured. "And you think I'll watch that happen twice?"

Their breaths collided, not yet kissing, but closer than sin.

And then the air snapped.

No Turning Back

Their mouths crashed like thunder.

It wasn't tender. It wasn't sweet. It was fire meeting gasoline, ignited by rage and history.

Valentina shoved him back into the wall, his back hitting the brick with a thud. His hands gripped her waist, dragging her flush against him. She hooked a leg around his hip, grinding down with intent.

Damien groaned—deep, guttural.

His fingers were everywhere, learning her. Her spine. Her ribs. Her thighs. Every inch of her claimed by a war neither of them wanted to stop.

She bit his lower lip, drawing blood. He kissed her harder for it.

Clothes peeled away, not carefully but out of need. Her shirt was pushed up. His belt undone with a vicious tug. The alley was forgotten.

The danger, the mission—irrelevant. All that mattered was the heat.

Her nails scored down his chest. His mouth found her neck. They didn't whisper names. Didn't ask permission.

This wasn't love. It was survival masquerading as desire.

A reminder that they were alive.

She gasped as he lifted her, slamming her back against the wall with one hand tangled in her hair, the other gripping her thigh. Their rhythm was frantic, dirty, desperate.

It wasn't just sex. It was defiance. A stake driven into the ground between enemy lines.

When it ended, their chests heaved.

Damien's forehead rested against hers, the air too thick to speak.

She slid down from his grasp, clothes half-fastened, lips swollen, jaw tight.

"That doesn't change anything," she said, voice hoarse.

He didn't answer right away. Just watched her. And then, with that infuriating calm, he smirked.

"No. It changes everything."

She walked away before he could see her doubt. Before she could feel hers.

CHAPTER 10

- Silk & Snakes -

THE MUSIC WALTZED through the halls like a siren—seductive, haunting, threaded with secrets.

Valentina stood still before the mirror in her old bedroom, the silk gown slipping over her skin like sin itself. Crimson. The same shade her mother wore at her final gala before vanishing behind closed doors and whispered betrayals.

The bodice clung to her curves, the neckline a deliberate invitation—her father's choice, not hers.

She didn't need to see his fingerprints on the fabric to know this dress was a message.

The maid had buttoned the last clasp without meeting her eyes. She was escorted to the ballroom by two guards dressed in tuxedos, their expressions blank but their eyes alert.

Outside, the estate shimmered with opulence: chandeliers of Venetian crystal hung like upside-down cathedrals, the scent of jasmine and blood-orange perfumes wafting through the air.

The guests were cloaked in masks and intentions. Marco Russo did not host parties; he orchestrated power.

From the top of the staircase, Valentina paused. Below, predators in gowns and tailored suits danced and drank beneath golden light.

Every smile was a lie. Every gaze a calculation.

Her father waited at the bottom, dressed in midnight black. He extended his hand like a king to his heir.

"The prodigal princess arrives," he murmured, guiding her to the ballroom floor.

"They've been waiting to see if the fire still burns in your blood."

She didn't answer. She didn't need to. Her silence was its own kind of rebellion.

Dance of Daggers

Masked faces turned toward her as she crossed the marble floor, each set of eyes dissecting, weighing, wanting. Among them stood one man in particular—tall, ruthless, crowned in Bratva arrogance.

Mikhail Volkov. The Bratva heir. Silver wolf mask. Sapphire cufflinks. A predator disguised as nobility.

She curtsied out of etiquette, not respect. He extended a hand with a smirk made for cruelty.

"You're more exquisite than I imagined," he said in Russian, his accent precise. "And more dangerous."

"I'm not yours," she replied coolly, letting him lead her into a waltz.

"Not yet."

His hand pressed against the small of her back, the other guiding her through the rhythm. To the world, they were poetry. In truth, it was a duel.

"You'll wear my ring, Valentina," he murmured close to her ear. "And bear my heirs. It is already decided."

Her lips curled slightly. "Let me guess. A strategic alliance for power and protection. How poetic."

He spun her. Her gown flared like fire. Her mask caught the light, casting shadow across her cheekbones.

"Not poetic," Mikhail said. "Profitable."

She didn't reply. Instead, she scanned the room—watching for patterns, guards, exits. But more than that, she searched for something else.

A flicker in the shadows near the wine bar.

A gloved hand adjusting a tray of drinks.

The staff uniform that fit too tightly on broad shoulders.

Damien. Watching.

Heat curled in her stomach. She turned back to Mikhail with a blade behind her smile.

"You want obedience, Mikhail?" she whispered as they slowed to a stop.

"You'll need a leash made of steel."

He chuckled. "Darling, I prefer chains."

Serpent and Rose

The party bled into the early hours, masks half-forgotten, laughter growing sharper with each sip of champagne.

Valentina slipped away under the guise of fatigue, her heels echoing softly against stone as she descended into the ancient wine cellar beneath the estate.

Here, the walls whispered.

Cobwebs clung to carved arches. Dust coated vintage bottles worth more than blood. And in the far corner, untouched by time, a mural stretched across the brick. Her mother's mural.

Painted before she died. Or disappeared. Or both.

A blooming rose—its petals open, curling into spirals. A serpent coiled beneath, fangs bared. The serpent was almost hidden, woven into the vines.

Only a careful eye would spot it.

Her fingers traced the paint, now dry and cracked. Her mother used symbols. Secrets painted in oil and silence.

She crouched low, fingers brushing the bricks beneath the serpent's head.

Click.

A tiny compartment shifted open.

Inside: an envelope. No name. Only a wax seal pressed with a chess knight.

And next to it, a folded scrap of paper. A note.

She opened it, her pulse quickening.

"Find the serpent under the rose."

Her breath hitched. She looked around.

Another hidden compartment?

Her eyes scanned the walls again—until she noticed it. The tile just left of the painting, chipped and worn, slightly different in color. She pushed it. It gave way.

A small velvet pouch fell into her palm.

Inside: a flash drive.

Encrypted files? A blackmail ledger? Secrets her father buried?

She didn't know yet—but it was leverage.

As she stood to leave, her burner phone buzzed once. A message.

Good girl.

She didn't need to ask who it was from.

Fury flared. And something else.

She pocketed the drive and slipped back toward the party. Back to the game.

Meanwhile, from a distant hill, through a high-powered scope, Damien's breath fogged the glass.

He wasn't here to shoot.

He was here to protect.

Through the lens, he watched her shadow glide through the cellar, saw the flick of her hair, the fierce grace of her movements.

He saw the way she stared down secrets like a storm.

"You're still playing," he murmured to himself. "Good."

She was fire. She was war.

And she was his, even if she didn't know it yet.

CHAPTER 11

- Grave Whispers -

THE CEMENTRY WAS quiet at dawn, veiled in the soft hush of mist. Marble angels stood guard over rows of the dead, their wings streaked with time.

Valentina stepped lightly over the gravel path, heels silent, dress trailing behind her like smoke.

She clutched a bouquet of white lilies—her mother's favorite. Not roses. Never roses. Her mother once said roses bloomed for the living, but lilies? Lilies whispered for the dead.

Her hand brushed the name etched in stone: Isabella De Luca Russo.

"No titles," she murmured under her breath. "Not wife. Not daughter. Not queen." Just Isabella. A woman the world tried to erase in pieces—until she disappeared entirely.

Valentina knelt, placing the lilies at the base of the grave. The cold seeped through her bones, but she didn't flinch. Her fingers lingered on the petals.

"I don't know who I am without you," she whispered, voice raw.

"But I'll find her. The girl you saw in me before the world turned her to steel."

The wind rustled through the trees, carrying the scent of damp earth and dying leaves. Silence followed, heavy but not empty.

She stayed like that for minutes. Hours. Time lost meaning here.

A faint crunch of gravel behind her—barely audible. But she knew it was him. The way the air thickened when he entered a space. The quiet violence in his presence.

Damien stood a few feet back, black coat buttoned to the throat, a single red rose in his hand. He didn't speak. Didn't offer condolence. Just lowered the rose onto the grave, his eyes flickering to the lilies.

"A red rose," she said, without turning. "Bold choice."

"She was bold," he replied, voice low. "And she tried to stop the empire before it swallowed her whole."

Valentina rose slowly, brushing off her knees. Her gaze met his, eyes still rimmed with unshed grief. "What do you mean?"

He exhaled. "She knew what Marco was becoming. What the Syndicate had already become."

Valentina's heart knocked against her ribs. "Then why didn't she leave?"

"She tried. For you."

His eyes darkened, like clouds before thunder.

"She came to Domenico. Begged him to take you both and run."

Her throat tightened. "Domenico said nothing."

"He couldn't. Because Marco found out."

The world tilted. A violent, silent spin.

Valentina took a step back. "You're telling me... my father ordered his own son's death?"

"I'm telling you," Damien said softly, "that he feared Domenico would tear the whole empire down. And your mother... she was collateral."

Her knees buckled. She sat on the stone bench beside the grave, the air thick with betrayal.

Damien didn't come closer. He gave her silence, let her drown in it.

Eventually, she looked up. "Why tell me now?"

"Because you're strong enough to hear it."

A beat passed. Then another.

"I hate you," she said, voice trembling. "For being right."

"I know," he said. "And I'll wear that hate like armor. As long as it keeps you alive."

Stormglass Hearts

The storm came in the evening—violent, electric. The kind that split the sky and flooded memories.

Valentina slipped through the halls of the estate like a ghost, unseen and unfollowed. She knew the guards' patterns now. Knew which floors creaked. Which doors stuck.

She found him in the old greenhouse, a place abandoned since her mother died. Ivy crept through broken panes, and the scent of rain mixed with roses long dead. Lightning lit the glass walls, casting Damien in fractured gold.

Neither spoke at first.

She crossed the room, steps slow but certain. He didn't move. Just watched her with that predator's calm—the stillness before a storm breaks.

"You're not supposed to be here," she said softly.

"I'm not supposed to want you either," he replied.

Silence fell again. But this time, it wasn't hollow.

Her fingers found the buttons of his shirt, undoing them one by one. Like a ritual. Like penance. His skin was warm beneath her hands, scarred and beautiful.

She pressed her lips to each mark, honoring pain, not erasing it.

He touched her like she was breakable. She touched him like she didn't care if they broke.

Their mouths met in slow-burning desperation. The kind of kiss that comes after truths too heavy to hold. There was no rush. No frenzy. Just need, unfolding like a secret between them.

She unzipped her dress, let it pool at her feet like spilled blood. He stared, reverent and ruined. Rain pounded the glass above as thunder rumbled.

They sank into each other like shelter. Her back met cold stone. His hands were fire. The world outside ceased to matter.

It wasn't soft. But it wasn't violent either. It was something in between. A claiming. A vow made in skin and breath and whispered oaths.

"I don't want to fall for you," she said, voice breaking against his throat.

"Too late," he murmured. "I fell the second you burned my name into your war."

They moved like dancers tracing the edge of a blade—every touch dangerous, every gasp a plea.

And when it was over, when their hearts beat in a broken harmony, she curled against him, breath shallow.

The storm outside softened to a hush, but inside the greenhouse, time stood suspended. Glass panes still trembled with the memory of thunder, their edges glistening with rain.

The air was thick with the scent of damp soil, roses long dead, and the faint citrus of his skin against hers. Somewhere between the ache and aftermath, Valentina lay with her head on Damien's chest, listening to the quiet drum of his heartbeat—steady, grounding, terrifying in its tenderness.

Neither of them spoke for a long time.

Her fingers traced the scar across his ribs, the one she hadn't dared ask about before. She felt the way his breath caught when she touched it, how his chest rose beneath her palm like a man who hadn't been held in a very long time.

"You're warm," she murmured, eyes unfocused, voice cracked from too many emotions.

"You thought I'd be cold?" he asked, one brow lifting lazily, but the husk in his voice betrayed the fragility under his teasing.

She gave the faintest nod, her cheek still pressed to him. "Cold. Calculating. Dangerous. The usual."

He exhaled through a quiet laugh, but it faded quickly. "I am those things. Just… not with you."

Her gaze lifted to his face—sharp edges softened by exhaustion and something deeper. Something that frightened her far more than threats or blood ever could.

"Why?" she asked. Not like a challenge. Just a woman asking for a truth she wasn't sure she could carry.

Damien didn't answer immediately. He brought her hand to his lips instead, kissed the back of her fingers. Not with seduction. But with reverence.

"Because," he said finally, "you make me forget that I was built for war."

She swallowed. There it was. The fracture inside her chest widened. She felt it—something dangerous and beautiful blooming beneath her skin.

"You make me remember that I'm not just a weapon. That there's a man under all this armor. And I hate it," he added, almost as an afterthought.

"I hate that I want to be better when I'm with you."

Valentina blinked hard, eyes stinging. She hated this too. This unraveling.

This need. This fragile, foolish hope that maybe, despite the blood on both their hands, they could be more than enemies pressed together by fate.

"We're both made of broken pieces," she whispered again, her voice catching on the edges of emotion.

He nodded, his hand sweeping a damp strand of hair from her face.

"Then let's make something sharp."

She looked up at him then, truly looked—and saw herself reflected back in the haunted storm of his eyes. Not the polished mask she wore for her father, not the ghost her brother tried to protect, not the woman Marco planned to auction off in a crimson gown.

But her. The girl who fought. The one who bled. The one who chose rage over silence and vengeance over fear.

"Something sharp," she repeated softly. "Like a blade forged in fire."

"Like a kingdom made from ashes," he said.

She leaned up, pressing her lips to his, but this kiss wasn't lust. It was acknowledgment. An understanding forged in silence.

Whatever they were—whatever they were becoming—it wasn't safe. It wasn't smart. But it was theirs.

And as the rain trickled down the broken glass above, tracing crooked lines like a prophecy, they lay tangled in each other beneath the shattered greenhouse roof, two ruins reborn in the wreckage.

Not whole. Not healed.

But dangerous.

And sharpening, together.

CHAPTER 12

- The Arrangement -

THE FLICKERING MONITORS cast a pale glow across Damien's face as he leaned forward, eyes locked on the surveillance feed from inside the Russo estate. The timestamp glitched. Static rippled down the footage. But the image was clear enough.

Ezra.

Valentina's most trusted soldier. Her chaos and steel.

Meeting with Marco Russo.

Damien's jaw ticked. His thumb hovered over the volume control, knuckles white against the leather of his chair. He didn't need to hear the words to understand what he was watching.

The way Ezra leaned in, kept his hands visible, deferential. The glint of a silver envelope exchanged under the table.

Damien rewound. Watched it again.

Every damn detail.

He thought of Valentina's laugh—rare, sharp, real only when she let herself forget. He thought of how Ezra stood at her shoulder like a shadow that bled loyalty. And now?

Now he was watching that shadow flicker.

"Luca," Damien said into the comm on his desk. "Get eyes on Ezra. No contact. Just follow."

A pause, then a confirmation crackled back. Damien didn't blink.

Betrayal wasn't new to him. He'd been raised on it—taught to smile while sharpening the knife behind his back. But watching it coil around *her*? That ignited something primal.

She was threading a needle through hell for him. For Gia. For a world she swore she would never return to.

And her world was cracking from within.

He leaned back, exhaled slowly, and reached for his glass. The whiskey was untouched. He didn't drink when he was planning war.

And tonight, he was planning exactly that.

The Diamond Collar

Valentina stared at the crimson gown laid across her bed like a crime scene. The fabric shimmered with blood-red undertones, sequins catching the chandelier light.

A replica of the dress her mother wore the night of the fateful gala—the night everything changed.

The irony was cruel. She could almost hear her mother's voice in the mirror: *Don't let them gild your chains and call it love.*

Her hands trembled as she zipped herself into it. The bodice hugged her too tightly, like it knew it didn't belong to her. A stylist—one of Marco's new recruits—adjusted her earrings while Enzo loomed by the door.

"You'll be on Dmitri's arm tonight," he said without looking at her. "Smile. Be gracious. Be Russo."

Valentina gave a single, dry laugh. "And if I don't?"

He finally turned. "Then your friend Gia bleeds."

That was all it took.

She kept her face neutral, lips parted in something almost like elegance. But inside, she was screaming.

In the mirror, her reflection didn't blink.

They paraded her through the estate like she was a trophy already won. The Bratva heir, Dmitri—cold eyes and colder hands—offered his arm with the confidence of a man who'd already measured her for a wedding band.

"You clean up well," he murmured. "But you'll look better in white."

Valentina smiled, saccharine and sharp. "You'll look better in the ground."

He laughed, but the tension in his grip betrayed him. He leaned down, brushing her ear with a voice soaked in threat.

"Don't test me, *printsessa*. The deal is already inked. The only question is how much pain we go through before the kiss."

She didn't answer. Just turned her head slightly, enough for the press to catch her best angle as flashbulbs flared and champagne flowed.

The dinner began in the ballroom under chandeliers that looked like they cost more than most people's lives. Marco toasted alliances. Dmitri boasted about weapons routes. Valentina raised her glass and said nothing.

But inside her chest?

A firestorm.

Later, in the shadowed corridor behind the grand piano, she found a moment to breathe. A sliver of silence. Her fingers trembled against her hip where her burner phone was tucked into a secret slit in her gown.

She tapped once.

He knows.

She didn't sign it. Didn't need to.

The reply came seconds later, vibrating once, a quiet heartbeat.

I'll tear it all down.

The Watchman

From the rooftop across the estate, Damien watched her descend the marble staircase, one arm wrapped around Dmitri's. Red silk clung to her like danger. She moved like smoke, eyes heavy-lidded but alert beneath the golden mask.

He knew every inch of her body by now. Knew the strength in her thighs, the steel in her spine, the curve of her fury.

But tonight, she was pretending again. Wearing the Russo mask with elegance that made him want to break something.

Luca stood behind him, adjusting the thermal scope. "That's one hell of a red dress."

Damien didn't answer.

He was locked on the way Dmitri's hand curled around Valentina's waist—too tight, too familiar. Like he thought he had already won.

He didn't see the blades hidden in her smile.

Damien's finger twitched on the scope trigger, even though he had no intention of firing. Not yet.

"She's walking into a den of wolves," he said quietly, voice like gravel.

"And I'll burn the forest to bring her back."

Luca glanced at him. "Orders?"

"Stay ready. When she calls it... we move."

Marco Russo's voice rang through the room, false pride wrapped around every syllable.

"Tonight, we celebrate a bond that will shape the future

of our families. The Russo-Bratva alliance will ensure peace, prosperity, and power for generations."

Applause.

Valentina didn't flinch. She sat at Dmitri's side, hands poised, back straight. Her face unreadable.

Only Damien would know how tightly her nails were digging into her own thigh.

Marco continued.

"And it is with great joy that I announce the engagement of my daughter—Valentina Russo—to Dmitri Volkov."

The cameras flashed. Guests rose. Glasses clinked.

And Valentina smiled.

It wasn't real.

Later, she would be alone in the powder room, tearing the diamond earrings from her lobes, staring at her reflection with something close to loathing.

But in that moment?

She owned the lie.

And Damien, watching from the shadows, understood the game she was playing.

She'd said it before: *I'll play bride. But the wedding will be a funeral.*

Now, it was time to start writing the guest list.

CHAPTER 13

- Pretty Poison -

THE BALLROOM glittered like sin. Golden chandeliers cast molten light over polished marble floors and men in tailored suits who smiled with sharpened teeth. Every surface gleamed, every flute of champagne sparkled, but the air carried a venomous tension—thinly veiled and perfumed in Dior.

Valentina Russo stepped into the room draped in crimson silk, the train of her gown a whisper of threat trailing behind her. She was the perfect vision of elegance, poised on the arm of Luka Volkov, heir to the Bratva throne.

A diamond necklace curled around her throat like a noose. Her smile—gracious, radiant—hid every blade she meant to bury.

This was her father's game. A performance of power. The Russo-Bratva engagement was the headline act, and she, the unwilling star.

Marco raised his glass from across the hall, surrounded by dignitaries and devils in bespoke suits. Enzo loomed nearby, his eyes always on her—unblinking, coiled.

Valentina raised her glass in return, the curve of her lips never faltering. But inside? The war raged. Every breath she took was a calculated pause. Every laugh a softened bullet.

Tonight wasn't about celebration. It was about infiltration.

She pressed herself subtly against Luka's side as he led her through the ballroom. He exuded entitlement—drunk on legacy and liquor.

Every time his fingers brushed her back, she imagined breaking them one by one.

But she smiled wider.

Because the ballroom was filled with key players: cartel leaders in imported linen, Bratva bosses with ice in their veins, and international brokers she'd only read about in encrypted files. And all of them were here for one reason—power.

So she studied them like a queen marking enemies across a chessboard.

Every name, every accent, every discreet whisper across velvet gloves was filed into the fortress of her mind.

She was not a pawn tonight. She was poison in heels.

Champagne and Curses

An hour in, the real work began.

Luka grew sloppy with each glass of champagne. His grip on her waist tightened, and so did his tongue. The more he drank, the more he bragged. About territories. About weapons. About loyalty paid in blood and oil.

She indulged him, laughing at the appropriate moments, her lashes lowered like a demure bride. But her mind? Sharpened like a scalpel.

He leaned close, his lips brushing her ear.

"We're funding the entire Balkan drop next month. It'll be the biggest arms move since Crimea. Your father's got deep pockets."

Valentina's smile remained flawless. Inside, she felt ice spread through her veins.

"And what does that buy the Bratva?" she asked softly.

"Loyalty. Fear. You," he smirked, resting a heavy hand on her thigh under the table.

"Russo blood and Bratva steel. We'll be unstoppable."

She reached for her flute of champagne, sipped delicately, and considered whether it would be poetic enough to shatter the glass and use it on his throat.

Instead, she leaned in, brushed her fingers across his chest, and whispered, "That's a lot of faith for a man who can't handle his vodka."

He chuckled like she'd complimented him.

Later, in a shadowed alcove near the rear courtyard, he pushed her against a stone pillar, his hands rough and territorial. The orchestra played something classical and hollow as the evening slipped into cruelty.

Her body tensed, not in fear but in calculation. One wrong move, and she'd blow her cover. One right move, and she'd own the night.

She tilted her head, let him think he'd won, then slid her hand into the inside of his coat. Her fingers closed around a metal keycard.

"Touch me again," she whispered against his ear, voice laced with honey and arsenic, "and I'll carve your name into my heel."

Luka blinked, stunned. His body stiffened as she slid out from under his arm, untouched but far from powerless.

By the time she returned to the main hall, she had what she needed. And Luka would remember her threat every time he looked at the mark she left with her stiletto's pointed edge.

The suite she was given on the third floor was cold—high ceilings, regal drapes, a carved oak desk that belonged in a museum.

Valentina locked the door behind her, kicked off her heels, and pulled her hair from its pinned coils with shaking fingers.

The room held its breath as she inserted the keycard into the burner decryptor hidden in her vanity drawer.

Lines of code flickered on the screen. Then—images.

Photographs of high-ranking officials. Missile coordinates. Bank accounts spanning Geneva, Istanbul, Singapore. It was not just a deal. It was a network—sprawling, ruthless, and soaked in blood.

Her hands stilled.

This wasn't just about her father anymore. This wasn't about avenging Domenico or burning Damien. This was about war. Not the poetic kind whispered in mafia poetry, but a global collapse kind of war.

The kind that bled into the cracks of society and turned borders into body counts.

She stared at the screen for a long time. Then she picked up the burner phone hidden in the lining of her suitcase.

Text to Damien: Your war? It just got global.

Seconds later, the phone buzzed.

Damien: Tell me what you see.

She hesitated. The words wouldn't come.

Because what she saw was too big for one message. Too devastating for one night. But beneath it all, she saw something else—something lethal and inevitable.

The truth.

The Russo empire was just one head of the hydra. And her blood? It ran through its veins.

She looked at herself in the antique mirror—makeup smudged, lipstick worn, her mother's diamond earrings still catching the light. A bride in red. A daughter born of legacy and fire. A traitor, or a savior. The line had blurred long ago.

Valentina pressed her fingertips to her reflection.

"Let the poison work," she whispered. "From the inside out."

CHAPTER 14

- The Wolf's Lie -

THE WAREHOUSE STANK of rust and gasoline, soaked into the bones of the place like an old betrayal. Fluorescent lights buzzed overhead—flickering, stuttering—casting jagged shadows across cracked concrete and crates filled with Syndicate contraband.

It was the kind of place men disappeared in. The kind of place no one screamed.

Damien stood in the center of it all, jaw locked, breath a low simmer in his chest. The pistol in his hand felt heavier than usual, like it understood the gravity of what he was about to do.

Footsteps echoed.

Ezra stepped into the light with his hands half-raised, not cocky—but not afraid either. His leather jacket was unzipped, revealing no weapons. His face was too calm.

"You brought me here to kill me?" he asked, voice hollow like the echo of a friendship that never was.

"I brought you here for the truth," Damien said coldly. "You owe her that much."

Ezra snorted. "You think I betrayed Valentina? You're the one dragging her into your blood games."

Damien didn't flinch. "You met with Marco. You gave him intel. And you didn't tell her."

"I was protecting her," Ezra snapped. "You don't get it, Moreau. You're not from her world. You don't know what Marco is capable of. I was born in that fire. I know how to breathe in the smoke."

Damien stepped closer, gun still aimed. "And lying to her is your way of keeping her safe?"

"She would've run headfirst into a bullet if she knew what was coming." Ezra's voice cracked. "I was buying time. Gathering proof. You came along and turned everything into chaos."

The silence between them was taut as a blade.

"Do you love her?" Damien asked.

Ezra's eyes flared. "That's none of your business."

"It is," Damien said softly, dangerously, "because I do."

Ezra lowered his hands but didn't move. His face twisted with old memories that seemed to cut sharper than the threat of a bullet.

"We were kids," he said, voice suddenly quieter. "After her mother died, Valentina was... hollow. Cold. But I saw the cracks. I knew how to make her laugh again. Knew how to keep her from falling into Marco's grip."

He stared past Damien like he was seeing something long gone. "I used to sneak her out through the servant tunnels. We'd climb to the chapel roof just to feel like the sky belonged to us. I was the one who taught her to hotwire her first car. She trusted me before she trusted anyone."

Damien's jaw clenched.

Ezra looked back at him. "And then you came in with your sniper eyes and your war plans. You think you're saving her? You're dragging her deeper."

"I'm giving her a way out."

"You're giving her a new kind of cage. One made of your blood and your enemies."

Damien didn't deny it. He just stepped forward until the muzzle of the gun pressed against Ezra's chest, right over his heart.

"If you ever betray her again," Damien said, low and final, "you won't walk away. You won't beg. You'll just stop breathing. Understand?"

Ezra met his eyes and, for once, said nothing.

What Loyalty Costs

The decision hit Damien the moment he walked into the surveillance vault.

It wasn't hard to find—the servers were stored in a side building off Syndicate grid, their contents encrypted, their footage damning. One drive held the recordings of Valentina sneaking messages out, disabling feeds, swiping keys from Bratva guards.

Another showed Ezra, alone, meeting Marco in a chapel corridor two nights before the engagement dinner. No audio. Just body language. And guilt.

Any of it could unravel her alliance. One leak, and she'd be dead before she could speak.

Damien loaded the drives into a burn canister.

The flame took quickly. Blue, white, then orange.

He stood there watching it eat away the evidence—of treachery, of loyalty, of everything that could be used to destroy her.

Ezra might've acted from fear. From jealousy. From a warped kind of love. But Damien? His loyalty came with fire. And fire left nothing behind.

When the last drive curled into ash, Damien stood in the smoke and let his shoulders drop for the first time in days. The war was shifting. Alliances were fraying.

But he would not let them touch her.

He walked out of the vault, the scent of fire still clinging to his coat, and sent a single message to her burner:

"Your secret stays yours. The rest I'll handle."

And somewhere, across the dark distance between them, he knew she would read it and understand.

Because trust didn't come in words. It came in the silences between threats. In the things you destroyed to protect the one person you couldn't afford to lose.

Damien Moreau didn't believe in mercy.

But for Valentina Russo?

He'd burn the whole world quiet.

CHAPTER 15

- Smoke & Skin -

VALENTINA FOUND THE bottle tucked between the Barolo and the Bordeaux. Crystal green, vintage. It didn't belong on that shelf—too old, too simple—and that alone made it suspicious.

She pulled it down with a frown and turned it in her hands.

The glass was cold, damp from condensation. Inside, rolled parchment sealed with red wax. No name. Just a sliver of a symbol stamped into the wax—an ouroboros, the serpent devouring its own tail.

She cracked the seal with her thumb, heart beating louder than the ballroom jazz that filtered through the cellar walls.

Midnight. Rooftop. Come alone.

Her breath hitched. The penmanship was angular, unmistakable. Damien Moreau's command came wrapped in elegance and ruin, like always.

She leaned back against the stone wall, the wine racks surrounding her like a cage made of luxury.

Her hands trembled, but not from fear.

This wasn't a summons.

It was a dare.

Under the Stars, Under the Skin

The rooftop stretched quiet above the estate, cloaked in shadows and ivy. Marble columns framed the night sky like a forgotten cathedral, and moonlight poured over everything—cold, silver, indifferent.

He was already there.

Damien stood with his back to her, jacket slung over one shoulder, shirt undone at the collar. The wind toyed with the hem of his black dress shirt, lifting it slightly, like even the night air wanted to touch him.

"You shouldn't be here," Valentina said, stepping out from the shadows.

He didn't turn. "Neither should you."

Something about his voice sent heat racing down her spine. It wasn't anger—it was restraint, coiled like a fuse begging for flame.

She walked closer, her heels silent on the stone. "This is insane, you know. You hiding in my father's home like a ghost."

His reply was soft. "I've always been a ghost to you."

That silenced her. The distance between them was shrinking and sharpening all at once. Moonlight struck his face as he turned, revealing a new scar just above his jawline—thin, recent. A reminder of the war they were both trying to win.

"You came," he said.

"I shouldn't have," she answered.

"But you did."

Silence again. It hung between them like the edge of a blade. Then she stepped forward and shoved him—not hard, but enough.

He didn't flinch.

"You don't get to be angry with me," she hissed. "Not after

everything. Not when you're the one who made me—"

His hands were on her wrists in a blink. Firm. Not rough.

"Why?" he asked, voice low. "Because I love you?"

She froze.

Time seemed to collapse inward.

The wind roared. Somewhere in the distance, a dog barked. Inside the house below, crystal laughed in clinking glasses.

"Say it," she whispered.

Damien stared at her, the rawness in his eyes undoing every wall she'd built since she was seventeen.

"I love you," he said. "I love you and I hate that I do. But it's the one goddamn thing I know is real."

Her mouth was on his before he finished the sentence.

The kiss wasn't soft. It was brutal—teeth, breath, broken syllables between mouths. Her back hit the stone column and his hands caged her in, braced on either side of her face. He tasted like the fire she'd lit in his world and the smoke he'd learned to breathe to survive it.

He lifted her, one fluid motion, and her legs wrapped around his waist. They weren't gentle. They were made of molten steel and past sins.

Her dress bunched around her hips. His mouth trailed fire down her neck. When his fingers touched skin, she gasped—not from surprise, but from how precisely he knew her, even now.

Damien pushed aside the fabric, one strap sliding off her shoulder like it had been waiting for years.

"Tell me to stop," he murmured against her skin.

"I'd rather die," she said, grabbing his belt.

That broke something inside him.

They crashed to the stone floor—her riding him like she was punishing every breath he'd taken without her. Her hips moved with violent grace, a rhythm only she knew. He gripped her thighs like a lifeline, his other hand tangled in her hair.

She bent forward, lips brushing his ear.

"Say it again."

He did. Again. And again. Each time between broken groans and reverent kisses. The wind howled around them, but it couldn't touch them.

They were heat and rage and love carved from ruin.

Clothes hung off them like afterthoughts. Her fingers roamed his chest, trailing over old scars, new wounds, and the one place his heart beat too loud.

She kissed that spot.

Damien choked on a sound he hadn't made in years.

And when they came undone together, it wasn't just sex—it was surrender. A mutual annihilation.

The rooftop was quiet now, but it wasn't peace—it was aftermath. That sacred, pulseless lull that follows fire when all that's left is smoke and breath.

Valentina lay sprawled across Damien's chest, her hair tangled against his skin, slick with heat and salt. The cold marble beneath them had long lost its bite, softened by the blaze of their bodies.

His coat draped across her back, too big, too masculine—yet it enveloped her like safety. Like a claim.

The city sprawled around them below, glittering and oblivious. The stars overhead blinked indifferent. But up here, on this rooftop of war and ruin, something unspoken had shifted. Something irreparable.

She listened to his heartbeat. Slow now. Steady. Like hers. As if, just for tonight, their clocks had finally synced.

"I've never..." she began, voice barely a breath, "...felt like this."

He didn't respond with words, only pulled her closer. His fingers traced idle circles over her bare spine, calloused touch soft as silk.

It was strange—how a man who could kill without hesitation could also hold her like she was glass.

Valentina tilted her head to look up at him. In the silver light, he looked younger. Not softer—he would never be soft—but stripped of his armor, at least for now.

"What are you thinking?" she whispered.

Damien exhaled slowly. "That I wish we had more time."

She frowned, propping herself up on one elbow. "We do."

He shook his head. "Not really. Every second I'm here, I risk exposing you. If they catch wind—"

"Then let them," she said, a sudden ferocity cutting through her quiet.

"Let them try."

He looked at her then, truly looked—like she was a miracle he didn't believe in but couldn't deny anymore.

His hand came up to cradle her cheek, thumb brushing the corner of her mouth, still swollen from their kisses.

"You scare me, Valentina."

She blinked. "Why?"

"Because you make me want things I was trained to destroy."

Her throat tightened. She leaned down and kissed him again —softer this time. A vow made in silence.

They didn't speak for a long while after that. They didn't need to. The warmth between them was no longer frantic, no longer built on fury or fear. It was something gentler, deeper. The kind of heat that lingered under the skin long after the fire was gone.

At some point, she shifted, laying beside him rather than atop him, her fingers intertwined with his.

"You know," she said, voice thoughtful, "I used to dream about running away. Not to someone. Just... away."

He turned his head toward her. "And now?"

She met his eyes. "Now I dream of burning it all down."

He smirked. "That's my girl."

She laughed, low and bitter. "Don't romanticize it. I'm not yours, Damien."

His expression didn't change, but something flickered in his gaze—some wounded thing, ancient and familiar. He leaned in, lips brushing her ear.

"Not yet."

The words vibrated against her skin, dangerous and devastating.

The sky above them shifted—storm clouds creeping in from the west. Thunder rumbled in the distance, faint but ominous.

She sat up, pulling his coat tighter around her naked frame. "We should go."

He reached for his shirt and slid it on without breaking eye contact. "I'll leave first. You wait five minutes, then head down."

Valentina nodded, but didn't move. The weight of reality was already settling back onto her shoulders—names, threats, secrets. She would have to face Luka again. Wear the mask. Play the pawn.

But not tonight.

Not for five more minutes.

Damien stepped toward her one last time, hands cupping her face. He kissed her forehead, reverent and final. Like he knew something she didn't.

"When this is over," he murmured, "when the smoke clears... I want a life with you."

Her breath caught.

"Then fight like hell," she whispered.

CHAPTER 16

Blood In Wine

THE INVITATION ARRIVED laced with pretense. Gilded edges, a blood-red wax seal bearing the twisted sigil of the cartel. Inside, the script was elegant, almost romantic, but Valentina knew better. A private wine tasting at the villa's west wing—intimate, exclusive, and lethal in all the ways that mattered.

She wore deep burgundy silk that molded to her like intention, hair swept into a sleek twist that showed the cold angle of her jaw. Every detail calculated. Every move rehearsed.

The poison nestled in the satin lining of her glove case was called *noctis*. Slow, undetectable, fatal within seventy-two hours. It mimicked natural causes. The perfect assassin's whisper.

She arrived precisely three minutes late.

Candles flickered. Decanters gleamed. Around the tasting table sat men who had bought cities and burned continents. At the center, Don Rafael Vasquez—the aging serpent whose cartel had smuggled death in barrels of Malbec and sold nightmares by the crate.

Valentina met his gaze and smiled. "A pleasure, Don Rafael."

He stood to kiss her hand. "The pleasure, Signorina Russo, is entirely mine."

A lie. Everything here was.

She took her seat, third from the head, where the server—her contact—would bring the poisoned glass. It came, as promised, during the second pour. A 2003 Chianti. Bold. Acidic. Full of secrets.

As she raised it, her fingers barely trembled.

Don Rafael sniffed, sipped, and hummed. She mirrored him, letting the tainted wine roll across her tongue before swallowing with a serene smile.

Inside, her pulse thudded once—hard.

The Serpent's Mouth

Conversation slithered. Wine softened their tongues. They spoke of markets and shipments, ports compromised and officials bought like street fruit. Valentina laughed at all the right jokes, her smile radiant, her interest modest.

But beneath the table, she activated the listening device sewn into her clutch, transmitting every syllable.

When the sommelier reached for the crystal decanter of Malbec, her fingers brushed it too—just long enough to slip the second bug beneath its base. It clung invisibly, a spider in a nest of serpents.

Don Rafael leaned close.

"Your father," he said softly, "has ambition. But ambition without brutality is just a wish. Do you understand that, *bella regina*?"

She let her eyes narrow just slightly. "I understand many things, Don Rafael."

Like the way your liver will fail in sixty-eight hours. Like the last thing you'll taste will be tannins and regret.

From across the room, Enzo's gaze pierced her. Sharp. Suspicious. He didn't drink. Didn't joke. His hands were still, his smile absent.

She caught the scent of danger in him before he even rose from his chair.

She reached her bedroom five minutes before he followed.

The knock came sharp. Demanding.

She answered in a silk robe, tied low on her hips, and an expression like warm honey. "Enzo," she purred. "Couldn't stay away?"

His jaw twitched. "You're playing something, Valentina."

She stepped aside, letting him in. "Aren't we all?"

He entered without waiting. Checked the windows. The mirror. She let the robe slip just a little further from her shoulder. His eyes flicked—but only briefly.

She crossed to the vanity, fingers tracing the edge of her mother's old jewelry box, now hiding the second burner phone. His gaze followed.

"You've been different since you came back," he muttered.

"I've grown up."

He stepped closer. "You've changed."

She turned. Close now. Her perfume between them—jasmine, and something sharper beneath. "You don't like it?"

"I don't trust it."

"Then maybe you should drink with me," she offered, lifting a crystal glass already poured.

He hesitated.

She laughed softly. "Scared?"

He took it.

Within minutes, the liquor softened him. She whispered memories from childhood, half-truths spun like gold threads. Slid her hand across his thigh like nothing had changed, like they were still playing in corridors with stolen cigarettes and broken rules.

As his head lulled back, she leaned in.

"You want to know the truth?" she whispered against his ear. "You've always been easy to distract."

She took the cartel manifest from his coat while his eyes slipped shut.

Later that night, the villa was silent.

Valentina sat cross-legged on the floor of her bedroom, decrypting files from the stolen manifest. Missile schematics. Offshore accounts. Political targets. Names she recognized.

Names she'd buried. It wasn't just arms anymore. It was destabilization. Regime collapse. International warfare funded by Russo money and cartel blood.

Her phone buzzed.

Damien:
you're playing god now.

She stared at the message, her fingers resting on the keys. In the window, her reflection stared back—red silk, bare shoulders, and eyes that no longer looked like her mother's.

Her reply was slow. Steady.

no.
I'm playing queen.

CHAPTER 17

- The Judas Within -

THE SCENT OF SCORCHED metal hit her before the smoke did.

Valentina stood in the skeletal remains of what used to be Gia's safehouse—now just a carcass of blackened timber and glass melted into slag.

Her breath hitched, caught somewhere between disbelief and nausea as she stepped over the twisted threshold.

Charred photographs crumbled under her boots. A familiar throw blanket, singed but recognizable, lay discarded near the shattered frame of a bed. Gia had chosen this place for its anonymity—quiet, buried deep in the Serbian outskirts. It was supposed to be untraceable.

Yet someone had found it.

And made sure no one walked out alive.

But there was no body. No blood. Just smoke-stained silence and the kind of devastation that screams a message.

She reached into her coat pocket, fingers trembling as she dialed the encrypted line.

Damien answered on the second ring. His voice, cool but clipped, was an anchor.

"Tell me everything."

The Devil Sends a Message

They found the video an hour later. It was sent from a dead cartel domain—scrambled IPs, bounced through proxies, nearly untraceable. But the contents were unmistakable.

The screen opened to darkness. A wheeze of static. Then—Gia.

Bound to a rusted chair, her face swollen, blood at the corner of her mouth. Bruises bloomed across her skin like purple ink. Her sobs were quiet, restrained, as though she still feared being punished for them.

Valentina stopped breathing.

A figure stepped into frame—face masked, voice electronically distorted.
"She's alive. For now. Trade the files... or she won't be."

Then the screen cut to black.

Valentina slammed the laptop shut so hard the hinges cracked.
"No," she whispered, the word tearing from her throat like a blade. "No, no, no."

The room spun. Her knees buckled, and she caught the edge of the table to steady herself. Damien crossed to her in two strides.

"She's still alive," he said, voice low, hands catching her arms. "This isn't over."

But it already felt like a funeral.

The Doubt

Ezra swore he hadn't spoken to anyone. That he hadn't leaked coordinates, hadn't known Gia had even moved locations.

But Valentina saw the way he flinched when she mentioned the safehouse—too fast, too guilty.

She cornered him in the eastern wing of the estate. The hallway was narrow, dimly lit by the amber glow of antique sconces, but her rage illuminated every inch.

"You told them where she was."

His mouth parted in shock. "What—Val, no—"

"You're the only one who knew. You were there when I moved her. You watched me secure the file logs."

"I didn't give her up," Ezra insisted, his voice cracking like dry wood. "You think I'd sell her out? After everything?"

Her voice rose, ragged with fury. "I don't know what to think anymore! You lied about Marco. You lied about the meetings. Why not this?"

He recoiled, as though she'd struck him. And maybe she had—just not with her hands.

"I was protecting you," he said, quietly now, shoulders hunched. "I always have."

Valentina stepped back, heart pounding against her ribs like a war drum. For a moment, she didn't trust herself to speak.

Damien found her moments later in one of the shadowed halls, her hands shaking, her breath uneven.

Without a word, he wrapped her in his arms. Her head found his chest, and the scent of him—gunmetal, spice, and something grounding—was the only thing that kept her from unraveling completely.

"I hate this," she whispered. "I hate doubting him. I hate feeling this powerless."

Damien pressed a kiss to her temple, his voice iron wrapped in silk.
"We'll find her. I swear it."

The intel led them to the outskirts of Novi Sad—a derelict cartel facility hidden behind the guise of a meat-packing warehouse. The building reeked of iron and old blood, the kind of place where screams went unanswered.

Valentina's Glock was steady in her grip. Damien moved beside her like a shadow, wordless, lethal.

They moved fast—breaching doors, clearing rooms, searching every corridor. Her heartbeat rattled in her skull.

Then they found the cell.

Empty.

Too empty.

She sensed it a split second too late.

From the scaffolding above, gunfire erupted.

It all happened in the space between heartbeats.

One second, she was turning toward the flash of muzzle light—

The next, Damien's body collided with hers.

The force sent them both to the floor. She landed hard, pain ricocheting through her ribs.

Then she heard it.

The sound she'd feared more than anything.

A sharp intake of breath.

Blood.

Damien's blood.

He was on his side, one arm still around her, the other pressed to his abdomen—where the bullet had torn through muscle and flesh. His expression was unreadable, clenched in agony, but calm.

"Damien," she gasped, trying to sit up, trying to stop the red from pooling through his shirt.

"No. No, no, stay with me."

His lips moved, barely audible. "You're safe."

Valentina screamed for help, voice echoing off concrete walls. Ezra's voice crackled through the comms—backup was minutes out.

She pressed her hands to his wound, trying to stop the bleeding, trying to hold him together.

His eyes locked on hers—storm gray and unyielding. "I'd do it again," he whispered. "Every time."

Then his head tilted back, and the world went quiet.

Too quiet.

CHAPTER 18

- Hollow Girl -

THE STERILE BEEP of the heart monitor was a metronome to Valentina's racing thoughts. Each pulse of sound marked the rhythm of her anxiety, the crescendo of her fear.

Then, without warning, the beep elongated into a continuous tone—a flatline.

Time seemed to stretch, the world narrowing to the singular, unbearable sound. Her breath caught in her throat, a scream building within her chest, desperate to escape.

When it finally did, it was a raw, guttural wail that seemed to shake the very foundations of the room. Nurses rushed in, their movements a blur, but Valentina remained rooted to the spot, her gaze fixed on Damien's lifeless form.

The man who had become her anchor, her partner in a world of chaos, was now slipping away from her grasp. The reality was too cruel, too final.

She couldn't—wouldn't—accept it.

Words That Cut Deeper Than Knives

In the cold, impersonal confines of the hospital corridor, Marco stood before her, his expression a mask of feigned concern. His eyes, however, betrayed a flicker of something else—satisfaction, perhaps, or relief. He placed a hand on her shoulder, a gesture that felt more like a shackle than a comfort.

"I always told you," he began, his voice smooth, "love makes you weak."

His words were daggers, each syllable a wound to her already shattered heart.

She wanted to retort, to lash out, but the weight of grief anchored her.

Instead, she met his gaze, her eyes betraying nothing, her face an impassive mask.

Inside, however, a storm raged—a tempest of fury, sorrow, and a burgeoning resolve.

That night, Valentina retreated to her mother's study, the room heavy with the scent of aged paper and memories. The walls, lined with shelves of books, seemed to close in around her.

She moved mechanically, her actions devoid of emotion.

Her fingers brushed over the spines of childhood books, pausing on a collection of her early drawings—crude sketches of castles, dragons, and families. The innocence of her youth mocked her current reality.

With a sudden, decisive motion, she tore off her engagement ring, the cold metal clinking as it hit the floor.

She stared at it for a moment, the symbol of broken promises and shattered dreams, before turning her attention to the garment hanging in the corner—the wedding dress she had once envisioned wearing. Now, it was a ghost of a future that would never be.

She approached it with a sense of finality, her fingers gripping the fabric as she set it aflame.

The dress burned quickly, the flames consuming her past aspirations, reducing them to ash.

Emerging from the study, she was no longer the woman who had entered. Her transformation was not just physical but deeply psychological. She donned a crimson leather ensemble, the color symbolizing both her rage and her rebirth.

Her hair, usually cascading in waves, was now slicked back, exuding a sense of controlled chaos.

Her eyes, once pools of warmth, were now cold, calculating, reflecting the storm within.

She was a phoenix risen from the ashes of her former self, ready to wage war on those who had wronged her.

The Declaration of War

The hallway lights flickered as she walked, shadows bending around her like a shroud. Every step was a calculated echo, boots tapping a rhythm of war. The estate's silence was brittle, as if even the walls were holding their breath.

Servants froze when they saw her, unsure whether to bow or flee. None dared speak. Not with that look in her eyes.

Valentina Russo had been many things—daughter, pawn, lover, whisperer of secrets—but never like this. Never a weapon.

The crimson leather clung to her like armor, molded to the sharpness she no longer bothered to hide. Her hair, wet from the rain she hadn't bothered to shield herself from, was slicked back like a crown of blood.

She carried no gun. She didn't need one. Her presence was violence incarnate.

She strode past the dining room where Marco dined with cartel leaders, laughter thick as smoke. His voice rose above the others, charming, amused. He was celebrating a deal signed in blood and silence.

He hadn't yet heard what she had done—what she was about to do.

Valentina stopped just outside the doorway, standing in full view of the chandelier-lit room, her silhouette framed in the soft amber glow.

All eyes turned to her. Wine glasses stilled mid-air. Utensils clinked against porcelain as if recoiling from her presence.

Marco stood, his smile faltering. "Figlia, is something—"

She cut him off with a single glance. Cold. Regal. Dangerous.

"I'm not your daughter anymore," she said, loud enough for everyone to hear. "You made sure of that the moment you sold out my brother. The moment you tried to bury my mother's voice. The moment you dared touch what was mine."

His nostrils flared, a flicker of anger behind his false calm. "You're emotional. Sit. We can talk—"

"No." Her voice didn't rise. It didn't need to. Still, it sliced the air like a scalpel.

"You taught me something valuable, Papà. That love makes you weak. But now I've lost the only person who made me human. And what's left isn't weak. It's unbreakable."

The Bratva heir leaned forward, amused.

"Careful, Valentina. That sounds like treason."

She turned to him, eyes gleaming with the quiet joy of a serpent before the strike.

"Oh, Luka. You haven't even seen treason yet."

She reached into her coat and dropped a flash drive onto the table with a soft click. The men exchanged glances.

"That contains every file I stole from your network. Bank accounts. Kill lists. Arms shipments. Political blackmail. I've already sent copies to your enemies. And to every international watchdog with a grudge."

Marco's face drained of color. "You wouldn't."

Valentina stepped closer, her voice velvet-wrapped steel. "You should've killed me when you had the chance."

The cartel leader to Marco's left stood abruptly, gun already drawn. She didn't flinch. From the shadows behind her, Enzo emerged, looking pale and stunned.

He'd followed her. Heard everything. Seen too much.

She didn't even look at him. "You should decide quickly whose side you're on, Enzo."

He hesitated.

Then he stepped in front of her. Not to shield her. Not to protect her. But to bow his head in reluctant allegiance. The room rippled with tension, the fault line of betrayal stretching wide and ready to split.

"You'll start a war," Marco said, his voice low, desperate.

"No," she replied, her eyes never leaving his. "I'll finish one."

And with that, she turned and walked out—unhurried, unfazed. Behind her, voices erupted. Chairs scraped. Orders were barked. But no one followed. No one dared.

The night swallowed her whole as she emerged into the cold, damp garden where her mother once hosted galas beneath the stars. A place of elegance now drenched in the stench of power and corruption.

She stood there a moment, face lifted to the sky, letting the rain fall on her bare skin like a benediction.

Her phone buzzed.

A message from an encrypted number. Damien's backup team.

Ready when you are, Queen.

She smiled.

Not the smile of the girl she used to be—the one who laughed under chandeliers and hoped her father loved her. No, this was the smile of a woman forged by betrayal and carved by grief.

The hollow girl was gone.

What remained was a sovereign built of ash and vengeance, dressed in warpaint, and crowned in fire.

And she would not kneel again.

Not to blood.
Not to men.
Not to God.

Only to the war she had now declared.

CHAPTER 19

- Crimson Bride -

THE GRAND HALL was a vision of opulence, its marble floors gleaming beneath the soft glow of crystal chandeliers. Velvet drapes in deep crimson adorned the walls, and the air was thick with the scent of expensive cigars and the low murmur of conversation.

At the far end, a makeshift altar stood, flanked by towering arrangements of white lilies and black roses. The stage was set for a union that would reshape the underworld.

Valentina stood behind a velvet curtain, her fingers tracing the intricate patterns of her custom gown. The fabric was a masterpiece—crimson silk interwoven with black lace, designed to resemble war paint more than wedding attire.

It was a symbol of her transformation, a declaration of the battle she was about to wage.

Her mother, Sophia, appeared beside her, adjusting the veil that cascaded over Valentina's raven-black hair.

"You look every bit the queen you're destined to be," Sophia remarked, her voice tinged with pride and sorrow.

Valentina met her mother's gaze, her eyes steely.

"Today, I reclaim what's mine."

The procession began. Valentina stepped onto the aisle, her heels clicking with each deliberate stride. On either side, cartel leaders and their entourages stood, their eyes following her every move.

At the altar, Luka awaited, his expression a mix of smug anticipation and concealed arrogance. Marco, her father, stood beside him, beaming with pride.

As Valentina approached, Luka's lips curled into a smile. "You look stunning," he said, his voice dripping with insincerity.

Valentina's gaze swept over the gathering, her eyes cold. "Let's make this quick," she replied, her tone devoid of warmth.

The officiant, a minor figure in the cartel hierarchy, began the ceremony, his words a blur as Valentina's mind raced.

She had orchestrated every detail, ensuring that this union would be both her ascension and her vengeance.

Moments later, they stood before their guests, glasses of aged scotch in hand. The room fell silent as Valentina raised her glass.

"To new beginnings," she began, her voice steady and clear.

"To alliances forged in fire and tested by blood."

A murmur of agreement rippled through the assembly.

"May our paths be illuminated by the lessons of our past," she continued, her eyes locking with Marco's. "And may we always remember that the brightest flames cast the darkest shadows."

She took a sip, savoring the burn as it slid down her throat. Luka mirrored her actions, his eyes never leaving hers.

They turned to face each other, and as their lips met in a kiss meant to seal their union, Luka's body stiffened. His hands gripped her arms, his face contorting in pain.

"What's happening?" he gasped, his voice strained.

Valentina stepped back, her expression unreadable. "You should have read the fine print," she murmured.

Luka collapsed, convulsing violently, foam bubbling at his mouth. The guests erupted into chaos, some rushing to his side, others backing away in horror.

Marco stood frozen, disbelief etched across his features.

Amidst the pandemonium, Valentina remained composed. She had anticipated this moment, orchestrated every detail with precision.

The lipstick she had applied earlier contained a rare, fast-acting neurotoxin, a compound she had acquired from a discreet source known for its lethal efficacy.

The toxin targeted the nervous system, inducing seizures and respiratory failure within minutes. Luka's demise was both a spectacle and a message.

As the scene unfolded, gunfire erupted, shattering the chaos. Valentina's allies, hidden among the guests, revealed themselves, their weapons drawn.

They moved with practiced efficiency, disarming guards and neutralizing threats. The cartel leaders, once untouchable, now found themselves vulnerable, their plans unraveled by the very woman they had underestimated.

Valentina walked slowly, deliberately, through the chaos. Her heels clicked with each step, a metronome marking the end of one era and the beginning of another.

Behind her, the hall descended into turmoil, the sounds of conflict blending with the crackling of flames that had begun to consume the structure.

The fire, set deliberately, spread quickly, its heat a reflection of the fury she had unleashed.

As she reached the exit, she turned, her gaze sweeping over

the destruction she had wrought. The building, her father's empire, was crumbling, reduced to ashes by her hand.

She whispered, her words carried away by the wind, "You should've let me choose love."

With that, she stepped into the night, leaving behind the remnants of her past and embracing the uncertain future she had carved with her own hands.

CHAPTER 20

- Firestarter -

VALENTINA STOOD AMIDST the inferno, her face splattered with blood—some her own, most from those who had dared oppose her. Yet, her expression remained impassive, a mask forged in the crucible of vengeance.

The compound that had once symbolized her family's dominance now lay in ruins, consumed by flames that reached for the heavens.

Marco barely escaped.

She had ensured his path was obstructed, her forces closing in from all sides. But the cunning patriarch had found a way out, slipping through the tightening noose. Enzo, ever loyal, had taken a bullet meant for Marco.

He now limped away, clutching his side, his face contorted in pain and fury.

Valentina did not chase—not yet.

She had orchestrated this night with meticulous precision, allowing Marco and his loyalists a semblance of escape. She wanted them to feel hunted, to experience the terror she had endured.

The predator had become the prey, and the hunt was far from over.

Days later, Valentina stood atop the hill overlooking the sprawling vineyards of the Russo estate. The once-thriving vineyard, now abandoned, bore the scars of neglect. Vines crept unchecked, and the grand villa at its heart stood in eerie silence.

"This place," she mused aloud, "was built on blood and betrayal. It's fitting it becomes our stronghold."

Her lieutenant, Marco's former consigliere, nodded. "The Russoni family were allies once. Their fall left this estate ripe for the taking."

Valentina's lips curled into a smile devoid of warmth. "Then we'll make it our own."

The estate's transformation began immediately. The villa's grand hall was fortified, surveillance systems installed, and hidden passages rediscovered. The vineyards, though wild, were cleared, and the land readied for future endeavors.

This would be her base, her command center, from which she would reclaim her empire.

Ezra's Return

Weeks passed, and the world began to feel the tremors of Valentina's resurgence. Her name became synonymous with fear and respect. Yet, amidst her growing power, a shadow from her past loomed.

Ezra had been her childhood friend, her confidant, and once, her betrayer. His return was unexpected, his appearance a testament to the hardships he had endured.

Bruised, weary, and carrying the weight of guilt, he approached the gates of the estate.

The guards hesitated but recognized him. Wordlessly, they escorted him to Valentina.

She stood in the courtyard, the morning sun casting long shadows. Ezra approached, his voice hoarse. "Valentina... I..."

She raised a hand, silencing him. "Save your apologies. Actions speak louder than words."

He dropped to one knee, his head bowed. "I failed you. I failed us. But I've come to make amends. Whatever you command, I will do."

Valentina studied him, her gaze piercing. "Loyalty isn't about love. It's about survival. Choose."

Ezra's eyes met hers, unwavering. "I choose you. Always."

She extended a hand, helping him to his feet. "Then prove it."

Mapping the Path to Revenge

The war room inside the reclaimed Russo vineyard estate was colder than it should have been. Not from the wind—though it howled outside, slithering through the old cracks in the stone walls—but from the silence inside.

A dangerous silence. The kind that comes just before a storm tears the sky in half.

Valentina stood alone at the head of a long oak table, her crimson coat draped over her shoulders like a shroud. Before her, a massive map of Europe stretched across the table's surface—creased, dog-eared, and bleeding with red ink.

Every mark, every pin, every piece of string was another name on her list. Another corpse waiting to happen.

She stared at it like a general surveying a battlefield. Which, in many ways, she was.

Dozens of cities were pinned in black—places where the cartel operated, where Russo money had been funneled into corruption, extortion, murder. Blue pins tracked movements of the Bratva. Green outlined former Russo allies now turned opportunists.

But it was the *red* pins that mattered.

Red meant blood.

Red meant betrayal.

Red meant *her*.

Her gaze stopped on the one circled in thick, violent ink: **Belgrade.**

She exhaled slowly. "That's where they're keeping her."

Gia's last known location. A cartel dungeon, encrypted and off-grid, nestled deep in Bratva-controlled territory. They thought it was clever, hiding her in the place no one would dare look—behind enemy alliances, behind a network of men who thought she was broken, discarded.

They were wrong.

Valentina's hands tightened around the edge of the table until her knuckles went white. The bruises on her ribs still ached. Her shoulder bore a fresh scar from the chaos at the engagement ambush.

Luka's death had sent shockwaves through the syndicate, but the war had only begun.

Behind her, the door creaked open.

Ezra stepped in cautiously. He didn't speak. Just watched her—still unsure of his place in this new world she was carving out with blade and flame.

She didn't turn.

"How many operatives do we have near Serbia?" she asked coolly.

"Four," Ezra said. "Two on the ground, two embedded in Bratva cells. But… we'll need more if we're going in hot."

Valentina finally looked up at him, her expression unreadable.

"We're not going in hot. Not yet. I want the building schematics, the power grid access, the names of every guard who took a bribe to look the other way."

He blinked. "You're planning something big."

"I'm not planning," she said. "I'm *promising*."

She turned back to the map, picked up a black marker, and drew a single line from Tuscany—where her estate now stood—through the Balkans and down into Belgrade. The path was jagged, like a scar.

"I want their entire chain of command exposed. We bleed them from the inside. Quietly. Then we strike."

Ezra approached the table, standing beside her, both of them watching the red circle like it might start pulsing.

"And when we find her?"

Valentina's lips barely moved. "We bring her home."

Her eyes glittered with something unreadable—something not quite grief and not quite rage, but something *older*, forged in the fires of everything she had lost.

"And Marco?" Ezra asked after a pause.

A cruel smile tugged at the corner of her lips. "He's not a target. He's the final act."

She opened a black folder and laid it out beside the map—photos of cartel generals, their wives, their sons, even their private residences. Everything she needed. Everything they never thought she'd find.

"This," she said softly, almost reverently, "is no longer about surviving. This is about *rewriting the rules.* They made me into a weapon. Now I'm going to show them what happens when the weapon chooses where to aim."

Outside, the wind howled louder. Storm clouds thickened over the hills.

And inside, the fire behind Valentina's eyes burned brighter than the vineyard's hearth.

Tomorrow, the hunt would begin.

But tonight, she mapped out their reckoning—slow, precise, inevitable.

Because vengeance wasn't loud. It didn't scream.

It planned. It waited.

It *remembered*.

CHAPTER 21

- Queen's Gambit -

THE DIMLY LIT auction hall in Vienna pulsed with an undercurrent of tension. Figures cloaked in anonymity moved gracefully among displays of illicit arms, priceless art, and, most disturbingly, human lives—paraded like luxury commodities.

Valentina, concealed beneath a raven-black veil and adorned in a form-fitting black dress that plunged daringly, navigated the opulent chaos with calculated elegance.

A slender dagger rested securely in her thigh holster, a silent testament to her readiness.

As she perused the exhibits, her gaze met that of a familiar, unwelcome presence—Madame Vorhees, a notorious broker of secrets and manipulator of destinies.

Their eyes locked, recognition flickering like a spark before it was smothered.

Approaching with a predator's grace, Madame Vorhees's lips curled into a serpentine smile.

"Valentina," she purred, her voice a velvet threat. "I never expected to see you here."

Valentina's response was a measured whisper, laced with a venomous sweetness.

"Life is full of surprises, isn't it?"

The air between them thickened with unspoken histories and mutual disdain. Yet, both recognized the potential in this encounter.

"I have information," Madame Vorhees offered, her eyes gleaming with calculated interest. "Gia's location. A small token for old times' sake."

Valentina's heart betrayed no emotion, her exterior unyielding.

"And what do you seek in return?"

"Intel on Marco's offshore accounts," Madame Vorhees proposed, her gaze unwavering. "The real ones, not the decoys."

Valentina's lips curled into a semblance of a smile, though her eyes remained cold.

"Consider it a deal," she agreed, her voice a silken promise.

The Bratva captain thought he was in control.

He sat back on the silk-upholstered chaise, cradling a glass of top-shelf whiskey, lips curved in a knowing smirk. "So," he drawled, eyes dragging over her curves, "what does the infamous Russo princess want from me tonight?"

Valentina didn't smile. She tilted her head, her dress a whisper of black silk slipping down one shoulder like an invitation wrapped in warning.

"You have access codes I need," she said, her tone velvet-clad steel.

The captain chuckled, cocky. "Is that what this is? Business? I was hoping for pleasure."

Her gaze turned lethal. She closed the distance between them with slow, deliberate steps, her heels clicking like a countdown. When she straddled him, he thought he'd won.

Fool.

Valentina leaned in, lips brushing his ear. "I always mix the two."

She kissed him hard—no softness, no seduction—just a bite of power. He responded, as expected, eager and drunk on her proximity. Her fingers tugged his shirt free, her thighs tightening around his hips.

The dagger hidden beneath her dress pressed against his ribs, unseen, unfelt—for now.

She unbuckled his belt with expert ease, her nails dragging along his skin like a promise and a threat.

"I don't like being touched without consent," she whispered against his jaw, voice like smoke. "So tonight, you'll follow orders. Or I'll leave you bleeding."

The captain moaned—part aroused, part afraid. It only made her smile.

She tied his hands above his head with his own tie, not gently, and rode him with calculated precision. Each movement was domination disguised as intimacy. Her breath hitched in rhythm with his until she leaned close, lips barely brushing his:

"Tell me the access codes," she breathed, right as he fell apart beneath her.

"Or I'll slice them out of your skin."

He gasped, stammering, but obeyed. Slurred numbers, a sequence she memorized instantly.

Then, with a practiced flick, she slid the syringe from her garter and sank it into his thigh.

His eyes widened. "What the f—?"

"You'll sleep for six hours. When you wake, you'll remember a fantasy, not a transaction." She kissed his cheek like a goodbye.

"Enjoy your dreams, Captain."

She stood, re-dressed in silence, stole his encrypted tablet from the dresser, and walked out without looking back.

Back in her suite, Valentina moved like a machine—her expression neutral, her blood still pulsing with adrenaline. She transferred the codes to an external drive, encrypted them with her personal cipher, and stashed the device beneath a false panel in her Louis Vuitton case.

She peeled off her dress in the candlelight, revealing the bruises the night had gifted her. Not from violence—he'd never had the chance—but from the constant pressure of pretending. Of performing.

She sat before the mirror and unpinned her hair. The woman who stared back was no longer the girl raised behind velvet gates and golden lies. No longer the obedient daughter, or the forced fiancée.

She was something else now.

A predator. A tactician. A queen with blood on her hands and no remorse in her heart.

Valentina opened her burner phone, typed in a message, and sent it to Damien:

Belgrade confirmed. I have the keys.
The hunt begins.

Then, with the moon washing her skin in silver, she leaned back in her chair, exhaled slowly, and whispered into the night:

"I don't need to win every move. Just the last one."

The city lights flickered far below her window like pieces on a chessboard—already shifting, already falling.

And Valentina Russo—crimson bride, daughter of the storm—was ready to end the game.

CHAPTER 22

- Resurrection –

POV: Damien

THE STERILE SCENT of antiseptic was the first thing that assaulted my senses as I regained consciousness. My body screamed in protest, each movement sending jolts of pain through my battered frame.

I tried to lift my hand to my face, but the effort was futile; my limbs felt foreign, disconnected.

"He's awake," a voice murmured from beside me.

I turned my head, wincing at the effort, and found a familiar face hovering near my bedside. Niklas. The realization hit me like a wave—Niklas, my old ally, had pulled me from the wreckage. He had saved me.

"Damien," he said softly, his hand resting on my uninjured arm. "You're safe now. You're in Montenegro."

Montenegro. The name sounded distant, foreign. My mind struggled to piece together the events that had led me here. The explosion. The gunfire. Valentina.

"Valentina?" I croaked, my throat dry, panic creeping into my chest.

Niklas's expression darkened, his eyes avoiding mine. "She's...

she's gone, Damien. We couldn't save her."

The words hit me like a physical blow. Gone. Valentina, the woman who had consumed my thoughts, my desires, my very soul—was gone. I felt a hollow emptiness settle within me, a void that threatened to swallow me whole.

"Where are we?" I managed to ask, my voice barely above a whisper.

"At a private clinic in Podgorica," Niklas replied. "One of the best in the region. They saved your life."

I tried to process his words, but my mind was clouded, foggy. The pain was relentless, a constant reminder of my fragility.

"How long?" I asked, struggling to keep my eyes open.

"Two weeks," he answered. "You've been unconscious for two weeks."

Two weeks. In that time, the world had moved on, and I had been left behind, clinging to the remnants of a life I once knew.

"Rest now," Niklas urged, his voice gentle. "You need to heal."

But sleep eluded me. My mind raced with thoughts of Valentina, of our plans, our dreams. Had they all been for nothing?

The days that followed were a blur of pain and confusion. My body healed slowly, each day bringing a little more strength, a little less pain. But my heart remained heavy, burdened by the loss of Valentina.

Niklas was a constant presence, his steady demeanor a comfort amidst the chaos of my thoughts. He filled me in on the details I had missed—the fall of the Russo empire, Valentina's rise to power, and ultimately, her tragic end.

"She was unstoppable," Niklas said one evening, his voice tinged with admiration. "A force to be reckoned with. But even the strongest fall."

I wanted to believe he was wrong. I wanted to believe Valentina was out there, fighting, surviving. But deep down, I knew the truth. She was gone.

Weeks passed, and I grew stronger, both physically and mentally. The pain dulled, replaced by a burning need for vengeance. Marco had taken everything from me—from us. He had to pay.

Niklas and I began to plan, gathering information, making contacts, building an army. We couldn't do it alone; we needed allies, resources, a strategy.

One night, as we pored over maps and intelligence reports, Niklas looked up from his papers, his expression serious.

"Damien," he began, his voice low, "there's something you need to see."

He handed me a dossier, thick with documents and photographs. I flipped through it, my eyes scanning the pages, until I found what he was referring to—a photograph of Valentina, alive, standing beside a man I didn't recognize.

"She's alive," I whispered, disbelief and hope flooding my senses.

Niklas nodded, his face grim. "But not in the way you think. She's with the Bratva, Damien. She's working for them."

The revelation hit me like a punch to the gut. Valentina, my Valentina, working with our enemies? It didn't make sense.

"Why?" I demanded, my voice rising. "Why would she do that?"

Niklas shook his head. "I don't know. But we need to find out."

The discovery set us on a new path. We couldn't just storm in guns blazing; we needed information, strategy, subtlety. We began to infiltrate the Bratva, posing as mercenaries, gaining their trust, learning their secrets.

Days turned into weeks as we worked our way deeper into their ranks. And then, one night, we found her.

Valentina stood in a dimly lit room, speaking with a Bratva captain. She looked different—hardened, colder—but it was unmistakably her.

I watched from the shadows, my heart aching at the sight of her. She was alive, but she was lost.

The next day, I confronted Niklas.

"We need to get to her," I said, urgency in my voice. "We need to bring her back."

Niklas met my gaze, his expression conflicted. "Damien, she's not the woman you remember. She's changed."

"I don't care," I replied, determination hardening my resolve. "I will save her."

We devised a plan to extract Valentina from the Bratva's clutches. It was risky, dangerous, and had a high chance of failure. But I couldn't let her go again. I couldn't lose her twice.

The night of the operation, everything went wrong.

We were ambushed, betrayed by someone we thought we could trust. Gunfire erupted, chaos ensued, and amidst the madness, I lost sight of Niklas.

I fought my way through the compound, searching for Valentina, calling her name. And then, in a small, dimly lit room, I found her.

She was kneeling, her hands bound, a Bratva soldier standing over her, a knife pressed to her throat.

"Valentina!" I shouted, rushing forward.

She looked up, her eyes meeting mine, and for a moment, I saw a flicker of recognition, of emotion. But it was quickly replaced by cold indifference.

"Damien," she said, her voice devoid of warmth. "You shouldn't have come."

I hesitated, confusion and hurt flooding my senses. "What happened to you? Why are you with them?"

She didn't answer, her gaze shifting to the soldier.

I knew then that she was lost to me, consumed by the very darkness we had once fought against.

I fought the soldier, my movements fueled by desperation and rage. I killed him, my hands stained with his blood, and then turned to Valentina.

"Come with me," I pleaded, extending my hand. "We can leave this life behind. Together."

She shook her head, tears welling in her eyes. "I can't, Damien. I'm not the woman you knew. I'm something else now."

With those words, she broke my heart all over again.

I left, taking Niklas's body with me, burying him in the place we had once called home.

Months passed, and I tried to rebuild, to find purpose , but nothing filled the hollow space she left behind.

Each night, I saw her in my dreams—sometimes covered in blood, sometimes barefoot in a white dress, sometimes laughing like the war never touched her soul. Always unreachable. Always fading.

Valentina Russo wasn't gone.

She had been *transformed*.

Not into a monster. Not into a martyr. Into something more dangerous than both—
A woman who had nothing left to lose.

And still, I couldn't let her go.

The first time I heard her voice again, it came through a

cracked comms channel intercepted by one of our tapped Bratva frequencies.

Her voice was lower, more measured. Colder.

"Prepare the ledger. Shipment route B is compromised. We switch to Montenegro route by dawn. And burn everything behind."

I stood frozen in the safehouse, the recording still echoing from the speakers. The others stared at me, waiting.

"That's her," I breathed. "She's calling the shots."

"She's not the Queen anymore," one of our men muttered. "She's the executioner."

They weren't wrong.

The Valentina on that recording didn't sound like the woman who had whispered *"I love you"* into my mouth under moonlight. She sounded like someone who'd been left behind, like someone who rose from her own funeral pyre and decided the world owed her fire.

I didn't tell anyone, but I followed the trail.

Every Bratva movement. Every cartel whisper. I traced the chaos—because it always burned in a pattern she used to design.

In Istanbul, I found a Bratva informant's body floating face-down in the Bosphorus.

In Naples, I uncovered a dead broker with a playing card lodged in his throat—Queen of Spades, folded down the middle.

She was leaving messages. Not for her enemies. For me.

The real twist came when I hacked into the Bratva's private vault database through a former contact in Odessa.

I expected coordinates, maybe offshore accounts. What I found was a video file.

Encrypted. Time-stamped.

File name: *Blackbird-Protocol-Valentina.*

I played it.

The screen opened to darkness. Then a click. A slow turn of camera focus.
And then—her.

Valentina.

Hair slicked back, blood on her collarbone, eyes calm. The fire behind her cast flickering shadows across her face like wings.

"If you're watching this," she said softly, "I'm dead. Or worse, I've had to become something you'll never recognize."

She exhaled. Then leaned closer to the lens.

"There was no other way, Damien. I had to break the world open. I had to destroy the system to free it. And if you think I've betrayed you... maybe I have. But it was the only way to save you."

I sat there, jaw locked, fingers trembling.

She was alive. But she was planning for the moment she wouldn't be.

And she was giving me permission—to hate her, to hunt her, to let go. But I wouldn't.

I closed the laptop. Sat back. And laughed once—dark, low.

"You think I'll stop now?" I whispered into the silence. "You think this is the end?"

No.

This was just the resurrection.

The mountains of Montenegro loomed behind me as I stepped onto the balcony of our temporary base, wind carving through my shirt. The map before me was littered with red pins. One stood out—**Belgrade.**

My chest burned.

The last known drop point for the Bratva's smuggling network. And likely—Gia's final prison.

I gripped the edge of the stone railing until my knuckles turned white. The world believed I was dead.

Let them.

They would never see me coming.

And when I walked through fire again, I'd walk with her name on my lips—not as a prayer, but as a warning.

Valentina Russo wasn't just a queen anymore.

She was the war itself.

And I was coming to reclaim what was mine.

CHAPTER 23

- Ashes to Ashes -

POV: Valentina

THE NIGHT WAS alive with the symphony of war.

Explosions reverberated through the air, sending tremors that rattled the very bones of the Bratva's Belgrade fortress. The scent of gunpowder mingled with the acrid tang of burning debris.

Shadows danced as flames licked the sky, casting an eerie glow over the battlefield.

I led my assault with unwavering determination, each step fueled by the singular purpose of reclaiming what was stolen from me. My team moved with precision, our synchronized movements a testament to years of training and shared purpose.

The Bratva's defenses, though formidable, were no match for our resolve.

We breached the outer walls, cutting down any who dared oppose us. The fortress, once a symbol of their power, now echoed with the cries of the fallen.

My heart beat not with triumph, but with a relentless drive to reach the depths where Gia was imprisoned.

Middle

The corridors of the fortress were a labyrinth of stone and steel, each turn a potential deathtrap. But I moved with purpose, guided by the whispers of informants and the burning need to reunite with my sister.

We encountered resistance—Bratva soldiers emerging from hidden alcoves, their eyes filled with fury and fear. But they were mere obstacles, easily dispatched by our superior tactics and firepower.

Finally, we reached the dungeon's entrance. The heavy iron door stood as a grim sentinel, its surface marred by years of neglect.

I signaled for my team to hold position, then approached alone.

The door creaked open, revealing a dimly lit chamber. The air was thick with the stench of decay and despair. And there, in the farthest corner, huddled a figure that made my blood run cold.

Gia.

Her once-vibrant form was gaunt, her skin pale and bruised. Her eyes, though clouded with pain, flickered with recognition as they met mine.

I rushed to her side, my hands trembling as I cupped her face. "Gia," I whispered, my voice breaking.

"I'm here. I'm so sorry it took so long."

Tears welled in her eyes as she reached up, her fingers brushing against my cheek.

"Val... I knew you'd come. I never stopped believing."

I pulled her into an embrace, holding her fragile body against mine. The weight of our separation, the years of torment, all melted away in that moment. We were together again.

She collapsed into me like a wave crashing against a crumbling shore—violent, breathless, unable to hold her shape.

Her body trembled in my arms, fragile as smoke, bones jutting sharply against skin too bruised to bear. Her sobs were not gentle; they were raw, animalistic, torn from the hollow of her chest as if they had waited years to escape.

I held her tighter, fingers digging into her spine, anchoring us both as I whispered the only words I could summon.

"I've got you. I've got you. You're safe now."

But safety was a myth, wasn't it? A word we tossed like a coin, hoping it would land face-up.

Her fingers clutched the fabric of my ruined blouse, bloodied and torn. "I thought you were dead. They told me you'd left me."

"I would never." My voice cracked, the sharp edge of guilt cutting through me.

"I never stopped searching. I didn't breathe until I found you."

She looked up then, and I saw her—not the broken shell, but the sister I remembered. Her eyes, rimmed red and glassy, held something feral, something surviving. "I kept hearing your voice... in my head. Telling me to hold on. That you were coming."

A tear broke loose and slid down my cheek, uninvited. I didn't wipe it away.

We rocked in silence, amidst the blood and ruin, two broken things clinging to the last thread of what made us human. It wasn't pretty. It wasn't triumphant. It was survival.

I kissed her hair, the same hair I used to braid when we were children. "They hurt you."

"Yes," she rasped.

"But not as much as I'm going to hurt them back."

There it was—the fire.

My hand found hers, fingers intertwined like we were sealing a blood oath.

"Then we burn the world together."

And just like that, the Queen in me bowed to the sister. The blade behind my ribs dulled.

The ice thawed, just enough to let grief pass through, and the promise of vengeance harden behind it.

The Detonation

Gia limped beside me, her body still frail, her steps unsure—but her eyes didn't flinch from the blood, or the wreckage, or the bodies of the men who once controlled her fate. She walked through it like a baptism. Born again in ash and fire.

We stepped out into the courtyard, the moon overhead full and indifferent, casting light on the inferno we were about to unleash.

Behind us, the Bratva stronghold loomed—scarred by the battle, but still standing. It wouldn't be for much longer.

I paused, pulling the remote detonator from my coat. The device felt heavier than it should have, as if it carried the weight of every scream Gia had swallowed, every nightmare she'd endured in silence. Every second we had lost.

"You sure?" Ezra's voice crackled through the comm in my ear. He and the others were already in position, waiting for my signal.

"I was sure the moment they laid a hand on her."

I looked at Gia. Her lips parted, breath shallow.

"They'll never hurt us again," I said, loud enough for the wind to carry it.

I pressed the trigger.

The explosion swallowed the fortress whole.

Fire erupted from the base of the stone tower, blooming upward in a cascade of light and heat. Walls buckled. Windows shattered. A second blast followed—the hidden cache we'd rigged beneath the east wing—sending a shockwave that rippled through the trees, flattening everything in its path.

It wasn't just destruction.

It was a cleansing.

The sky turned orange, painted with embers and vengeance. The night roared.

Gia leaned into me, her face blank with awe, lips trembling.

I didn't smile. There was nothing to celebrate. Not yet. But I held her as the ground quieted, as the flames devoured every last trace of the dungeon that had tried to break her.

My white blouse, soaked red, clung to my skin like a second scar.

When the silence settled, I whispered to the smoke:

"Let this be your grave."

Behind us, the team emerged, eyes wide at the scale of the destruction. But they said nothing. They didn't have to. Everyone knew what this was.

This was a declaration.

Gia's hand found mine again, tighter this time. Stronger.

"What now?" she asked, her voice still scratchy, but steadier.

I looked ahead—not just at the horizon, but past it. To Sicily. To Marco. To every man who ever underestimated what a woman could become once she had nothing left to lose.

"Now," I said, "we finish it."

And in the wake of fire and ruin, we walked—blood-soaked, bonded, reborn—not as survivors.

But as a storm.

CHAPTER 24

- Ghost in the Smoke -

THE VINEYARD ESTATE stood bathed in the soft glow of the setting sun, its rows of grapevines stretching endlessly towards the horizon. The air was thick with the scent of earth and ripening fruit, a stark contrast to the acrid smoke that still lingered from the recent destruction of the Bratva stronghold.

Valentina approached the grand entrance, her steps measured, each one resonating with the weight of her journey.

Inside, the estate hummed with activity. Her loyalists moved with purpose, their faces a mix of relief and anticipation.

Gia, though physically weakened, stood tall among them, her presence a testament to resilience.

Valentina's gaze met hers, and a silent understanding passed between them—a promise of protection, of family.

Later that evening, Valentina found herself alone in the garden, the tranquility offering a momentary respite from the chaos that had defined her life.

The moon hung low in the sky, its silver light guiding her steps as she made her way to the family mausoleum.

The path was familiar, each stone and plant a marker of her lineage.

Kneeling before her mother's grave, Valentina felt the weight of generations upon her. The engagement ring, once a symbol of a future intertwined with Marco, now felt like a shackle.

The knife, a tool of power and violence, had been her constant companion.

But in this moment, they represented a past she was determined to shed.

Placing the ring and knife atop the grave, she whispered, "I won't become him. Even if I must kill him." The words hung in the air, a vow to herself and to the legacy she was forging.

Returning to the estate, Valentina entered her private chambers, the door creaking softly behind her. The room was dimly lit, the only illumination coming from the flickering flames of the hearth.

As she moved further in, a sudden chill swept over her, a primal instinct alerting her to an unfamiliar presence.

Her hand instinctively reached for the drawer where she kept her firearm. Drawing it with practiced ease, she surveyed the room, her senses heightened.

The shadows seemed to dance, playing tricks on her mind.

Then, from the corner, a figure emerged—a man, tall and imposing, his features partially obscured by the dim light. Valentina's heart raced, her grip tightening on the gun. But before she could react, the figure stepped forward, into the light.

"Valentina," he rasped, his voice rough, as if unused to speech. "It's me. Damien."

Time seemed to stand still. Valentina's mind struggled to process the sight before her. Damien, presumed dead, stood alive, though bearing the marks of his ordeal.

Without thinking, she lowered the gun, her emotions overwhelming her. Damien closed the distance between them, his arms enveloping her in a tight embrace. The warmth of his body, the familiar scent of his cologne, grounded her in a reality she hadn't dared to hope for.

Tears welled in her eyes as she pulled back slightly to look at him.

"I thought I'd lost you," she whispered, her voice trembling.

Damien cupped her face, his thumb brushing away a stray tear. "You almost did," he replied, his gaze intense.

"But I couldn't leave you. Not like that."

Overcome with emotion, Valentina slapped him—not in anger, but as a release of the tension that had built up over their separation.

Damien's response was immediate; he pulled her into a kiss, deep and desperate, as if trying to convey all the words they hadn't spoken.

Their clothes became a distant memory, discarded carelessly as they rediscovered each other. There were no words, only the raw, unfiltered need to reconnect.

Their bodies moved together, a dance of passion and desperation.

Scars met scars, old wounds pressed against new ones, and for a moment, the pain of the past faded into the bliss of the present.

As they lay together, breathless and intertwined, Valentina rested her head on Damien's chest.

"Don't you ever leave me again," she murmured.

Damien's arms tightened around her. "You'd burn the world before I could," he replied, his voice filled with conviction.

They awoke wrapped in each other's arms, the first light of dawn filtering through the curtains. The empire awaited, its challenges looming, but in that moment, it was just the two of them.

Hand in hand, they faced the day, ready to confront whatever the world threw their way.

Together.

CHAPTER 25

- Bloodlines -

THE VINEYARD HAD been quiet since the fires—since Valentina tore down an empire in a single night. But silence was never peace. It was the sound of something loading, coiling, preparing to strike again.

Ash still clung to the walls. The scent of wine and gunpowder lingered in the cellar halls, soaked into stone, into skin. It was a place resurrected from ruin—her place now. She stood at the helm of what remained: a fractured empire, bruised but breathing.

Beneath the ancient arches, lit by oil lamps that danced like ghosts across cracked frescoes, the loyal had gathered.

Gia rested upstairs, sedated but safe. The bruises on her face had started to fade.

The ones beneath the surface, Valentina knew, would take longer. She didn't ask about the pain.

Didn't speak of what had been done in that dungeon. They simply held hands in the dark and said nothing at all.

Ezra lurked like a shadow just beyond the circle of light—gaunt, guilt-sharpened, and silent. Whatever he had once been—friend, brother, betrayer—he was now something fractured.

His loyalty, once absolute, now trembled beneath the weight

of secrets he could never take back.

Damien said nothing as he joined her in the courtyard, his steps quiet, purposeful. His presence was a constant now. No longer a ghost, no longer a secret to keep. He was bruised, healing, alive.

When their hands brushed, it wasn't romantic. It was a pact between killers.

Between survivors. Between the last two standing in a game where everyone else had been pieces.

There was no celebration. No champagne. No speeches.

Just silence, and strategy.

The world would think them weakened. It was their greatest advantage.

The Ledger of Ghosts

The safe had been buried beneath three feet of concrete and Bratva arrogance. Hidden in the decaying mansion outside Belgrade, locked behind biometric scans and fail-safes that only proved how much power the dead thought they would keep.

It took two blowtorches and Damien's bloodied fingerprint to get it open.

Inside, among stacks of rotting bearer bonds and uncut diamonds, sat a single black leather ledger.

Handwritten. Dated back two decades.

The ledger wasn't just numbers—it was confession. Trade routes. Shipment codes. Political payments. Death orders signed with elegant calligraphy.

Offshore accounts traced to Monaco, Dubai, the Caymans.

And at the bottom of nearly every page, one name repeated again and again.

Marco Russo

He hadn't just played the game. He built the table.

Ties to the Irish syndicates in Dublin. Gun corridors through Slovakia. Human trafficking contracts with the Moroccan networks. Bankers in Zurich. Weapons couriers in Serbia. Politicians on every payroll.

He hadn't planned to disappear—he planned to become untouchable.

But even kings bleed when the paper trail burns.

Word came through a coded message intercepted on an encrypted channel: Marco was in hiding, deep in the Dolomites, preparing to flee to Brazil.

He had a private jet, new documents, and fifty million in laundered assets moving through shell companies like serpents through sand.

Valentina traced the route on a map. Followed the red string from cartel hideouts to offshore banks to his last known fixer in Milan.

Damien watched as she circled the final destination—Sicily. The original Russo estate. Where her mother had once danced in silk and her father had drawn his first line in blood.

Damien spoke first, cold calculation behind the softness of his voice.

"If we wipe the accounts, the empire collapses."

Valentina didn't even look up.

"I'm not here for justice. I'm here for blood."

Return to the Wolf's Den

The sun sank low, bleeding copper into the Tuscan sky. The vineyard stretched in every direction—row after row of skeletal vines, bare from pruning, their twisted limbs reaching upward like the hands of the dead.

Spring had not yet returned, and the earth felt stripped, purged.

As if the land itself understood that something had died here... and something else was rising in its place.

Valentina walked alone through the uneven terrain, her boots pressing into the soil her ancestors once bled for.

The crisp wind dragged at her coat, carried with it the scent of cold stone, iron, and burnt wood.

Somewhere behind her, inside the estate, maps were being marked, weapons loaded, men positioned like pawns. But none of that followed her here.

This place was sacred.

It was the only ground she allowed herself to be unguarded.

Under the oldest olive tree, just past the final row of vines, sat the gravestone—small, unadorned, yet impossibly heavy with meaning. Her mother's name etched in delicate script: *Lucia Marino Russo.* No birthdate. No epitaph. Just the name, like an unfinished sentence. No one had buried her with ceremony.

Marco had made sure of that. Her body had been hidden, her memory erased, her blood swept under the mosaic floors of the Russo estate like a stain they didn't want to remember.

Valentina knelt, the cold dampness of the earth seeping through her pants as she reached into her coat. She pulled out three items, each wrapped in a black silk handkerchief. One by one, she placed them at the foot of the grave.

First, the engagement ring—platinum, blood-cleaned, now dulled by ash and memory. A symbol of control disguised as devotion.

Second, the stiletto knife—its handle worn, its blade still bearing the faint stain of a Bratva lieutenant's throat. The knife that had slit truth from silence.

And finally, the Queen of Spades card—edges scorched, corners curled. A crown she never asked for, but wore like armor anyway.

She sat back on her heels and stared at the collection, at the life she had dismantled and the one she was about to destroy.

"I came back, Mamma," she murmured. "But I'm not yours anymore. I'm not his either."

The wind stirred the grass. A few brittle leaves danced at the foot of the tree.

"I thought power would make me whole," she said. "I thought vengeance would be enough. But there's still something missing. A piece I buried with you."

Her voice broke, barely perceptible. "And I can't find it until he's gone."

She closed her eyes. Behind her lids played images like a reel of silent film—her mother's laughter, the sound of piano keys at dusk, the copper taste of her first bruise. Marco's voice barking orders through the halls. Damien bleeding on the marble floor.

Gia screaming in chains. It was all stitched together now, a patchwork of fury and failure.

"I won't become him," she whispered, her knuckles white on her thighs. "Even if I have to kill him to prove it."

She stayed there a while, until the wind calmed, until the moon rose in slivered defiance above the hills. Then she stood, left the offerings behind like sacred relics, and walked back toward the estate.

Inside, the war room had come alive.

Maps covered the entire dining table, overlapping like veins. Printed surveillance stills from Milan.

Travel logs from fake passports. Marco's financial escape plan, dissected and highlighted. Satellite footage of the Russo estate in Sicily—now quiet, heavily guarded, its outer walls reinforced with armed mercenaries.

Damien was there already, lit by firelight and candle smoke. He said nothing as Valentina entered. He didn't have to. He could read her the way others read code—line by line, scar by scar.

She took her place beside him, expression unreadable.

Ezra hovered at the edge of the room. His voice cracked the tension.

"There's still time to change the route. If we hit him in Milan—"

"No," Valentina interrupted. Calm. Certain. "This ends where it started."

She reached for the map, took a red wax pencil, and circled the location with brutal finality—Sicily. The place where the dynasty had been built on silks and secrets.

Where her father first learned how to weaponize love. Where her mother had died in silence.

"There's no more chasing," she said, loud enough for every loyalist in the room to hear. "No more waiting. No more mercy."

She looked up—eyes unflinching, voice as steady as a blade.

"He dies on Russo soil."

The room fell quiet. Absolute.

And the Queen of Spades returned to war.

CHAPTER 26

- The Last Supper -

THE LETTER ARRIVED on thick, ivory parchment, the edges torn by hand and the ink blotted like something resurrected from another century. No return address. No signature. Only a single line scrawled in looping, feminine script:

"One final meal. Come dressed for the truth."

Marco Russo read it in silence, his fingers lingering on the elegant loops of the handwriting he hadn't seen in years. He recognized it instantly. Not because he remembered it—but because he remembered her mother's.

The way she used to sign Valentina's birthday cards with the same kind of grace, the same slant of rebellion.

The daughter had inherited her beauty, but the vengeance... that was all his.

He didn't call his guards. Didn't alert his security detail. He slipped the letter into his breast pocket like a pressed flower, dressed in an old tuxedo that no longer fit his frame the way it used to.

Too much weight lost to paranoia. Too many sleepless nights unweaving decades of power, unraveling one stitch at a time, all because of her.

Outside, the car waited. A single driver. No license plate.

He climbed in without a word.

The road twisted in silence, carrying him to the broken heart of his own empire. The original Russo estate in Sicily. A place that had once echoed with ballroom laughter, smelled of his wife's perfume and the burnt sugar of childhood birthdays.

Now, it stood like a mausoleum carved from memory—ash on stone, silence on silence.

The iron gates creaked open on cue. The roses were long dead. The earth had turned bitter.

But the table—oh, the table was set.

A banquet stretched the length of the ruined courtyard, white linens fluttering in the windless dusk, flanked by flickering candles balanced on tarnished silver. Empty chairs stared like ghosts.

Crystal glasses shimmered with blood-colored wine.

And at the head of it all, she sat.

Valentina Russo.

Crimson silk curled around her like spilled blood, her hair pinned high like a crown forged in fire.

Her expression was unreadable—not blank, but deliberate. The stillness of a blade before the cut.

"Welcome home, *Padre*," she murmured.

The Feast of Ghosts

They dined beneath the Sicilian moon, its pale light fractured by the fractured stone arches that once protected a dynasty. Time hadn't softened them. It had sharpened every corner.

Valentina poured the wine herself, slow and steady. The ruby liquid pooled in both glasses as Marco studied her fingers—graceful, lethal.

"You always had your mother's hands," he said, folding his napkin with old-world precision. "Steady. Dangerous. A little too gentle for this world."

"She made them gentle," Valentina replied, her voice flat. "You made them dangerous."

Silence settled between them like dust on a forgotten portrait.

He sipped the wine, his throat tightening—not from poison, but from dread. She hadn't laced it. Not yet. That wasn't her style. No, she wanted him lucid. Aware.

She lifted her own glass, swirling it like a chalice in a ritual. "To endings," she said.

Marco matched her. "To blood."

Their toast echoed through the ruins like a final confession.

"You think this makes you strong," he said, trying for the calm he'd once wielded like a dagger. "But you're still my daughter. You carry my name."

Valentina tilted her head, amused. "You think names make blood sacred?"

"They make it *inevitable*."

She leaned forward then, the candlelight catching in her eyes like sparks behind glass.

"You killed the only legacy that mattered. The woman who gave me mercy when you only offered knives. The mother who died protecting a child from her own father's shadow."

Marco's jaw clenched. The past, for him, was a ledger: losses and gains, debt and silence. But for her, it had never been numbers—it had been wounds.

"And yet here we are," he said. "You, in red. Me, in black. You think this theater makes you queen?"

"No," she said softly. "I became queen the moment you

mistook my love for weakness."

He coughed—just once—and stiffened. His hand trembled against the stem of his glass.

Valentina said nothing. She just watched.

Panic flickered across his features, brief but raw. "What did you—"

"Nothing," she interrupted. "Not yet."

It was a lie. A masterstroke.

There was no poison. No drug. No toxin in his veins.

Only the idea of it.

And that, she had learned, was more devastating than the real thing.

He gasped for air that wasn't leaving him. His heartbeat roared in his ears, thudding against the ruins. The fear clawed up his throat, not from chemistry—but memory.

She had given him the one thing he had given countless others.

Powerlessness.

Valentina stood before him slowly, folding her napkin, the satin of her dress whispering against the cracked tiles. Around them, the candles flickered in the rising wind. Some extinguished. Some refused.

"I could have killed you," she said, her voice low, intimate, meant only for him.

"I still could."

Marco was trembling now, a man brought to ruin by the ghost of a girl he once shaped like clay. His voice cracked. "Why not finish it?"

She stepped close—so close her breath brushed his cheek. Her lips near his ear.

"Because death is a mercy," she whispered. "And I want you to live long enough to know you lost. That the empire you built on blood is crumbling brick by brick. That your daughter is the one burning it to ash."

She slipped something onto the table—a single Queen of Spades card, edges charred, stained at the corner with blood.

Her final calling card.

Then, without another word, she turned.

The courtyard stretched before her like a painting come undone. The wind curled around her.

The scent of wine and ruin clung to the air.

Behind her, Marco screamed—a sound that clawed at the stones, that echoed not with rage, but with the hollow terror of a man who had finally met his reckoning and found no god to save him.

Valentina did not flinch.

She walked into the vineyard night with her head high, the red silk trailing like war smoke, her heels echoing with the weight of generations—each step the punctuation of a legacy rewritten.

This was no longer the Russo legacy.

It was hers.

And she would end it the way it should have always begun:

With a woman, a crown, and a blade no man would ever dull again.

CHAPTER 27

- Hollow Crown -

THE NIGHT SMELLED like copper and gunpowder long before the first shot broke the silence. The vineyard estate stood bathed in moonlight—serene, regal, oblivious to the violence lurking beyond its borders. Then came the howling engines.

The crunch of gravel under booted feet. A hundred shadows moved like wolves in the dark, swarming the land with silencers, machetes, and bloodlust. Marco had come.

He sent no warning. Just death.

The first explosion tore through the north wall, shattering glass and dragging fire through the corridor like a devil's breath. The alarms didn't even have time to scream.

The house came alive—guns drawn, knives unsheathed, boots pounding against marble.

Valentina didn't flinch. She moved through smoke like a sovereign in her own hell, barking orders, her voice a whip through chaos.

Damien was already at the southern wing, blood on his hands, jaw set in stone. He fought like a shadow—silent, lethal, unrelenting. A former ghost resurrected for one final reckoning.

He moved between pillars, putting bullets through skulls without blinking, eyes always scanning for *her*—making sure the woman he died for wouldn't have to die again.

The air crackled with tension, fire licking the horizon. The estate, once a sanctuary of rebirth, became a battleground of memory and vengeance. Every hallway held ghosts.

Every room had seen too much. Now it demanded blood to balance the scales.

And the blood came.

The Cost of Loyalty

In the courtyard, beneath the crumbling archways carved with Russo insignias, Gia emerged like an avenging spirit. Her face was smeared with ash, her hair tangled in firelight, but her grip on the Glock was unshakable.

Enzo spotted her across the chaos, disbelief flickering through the rage in his eyes.

"You're just a girl," he snarled, raising his weapon.

"I was," she said softly, and pulled the trigger.

The bullet ripped through his chest, clean and merciless. Enzo collapsed, clutching his heart as if betrayal were something physical. Gia didn't watch him die.

She turned away before his final breath left his lips, the echo of vengeance too deafening to make room for mercy.

Inside, near the shattered dining hall, Ezra bled from a shoulder wound, eyes wide with pain and purpose. He stumbled down the hallway as the fighting intensified, drawn by a single instinct: protect the man who stayed when everyone else ran.

He found Damien just as a sniper's scope glinted through the window.

"No!" Ezra shouted, lunging forward.

The bullet found him first. It tore through his chest, brutal and clean. Damien caught him as he fell, as if time could be bent back into loyalty, as if one act of sacrifice could erase years of quiet betrayal.

"She always deserved better," Ezra gasped, blood bubbling at his lips. "Tell her... I tried."

Then nothing.

The war raged on, but in that hallway, silence took a knee.

The night was colder in the vineyard ruins. Wind slithered through the broken vines like ghosts returning to watch. Moonlight bathed the earth in a sickly silver hue, casting long, jagged shadows across the cracked stone paths that once led to feasts, to weddings, to whispered vows beneath olive branches. Now, they led to reckoning.

Marco staggered through the skeletal remains of the Russo estate, the place where it all began—where he built an empire of rot masked in grandeur.

His footsteps were uneven, dragged by exhaustion and dread, blood soaking through his shirt from a graze on his ribs. The air around him smelled of ash and iron, and in his lungs bloomed the first tremors of mortality.

He looked smaller now, less like a king, more like a man chasing the memory of power.

He turned toward the sound of her steps. Gravel under boots. Measured, deliberate, sovereign. Valentina emerged from the smoke without hesitation, as if she had always known he would come here—to die where he had once reigned.

She moved like a requiem. There was no rush in her gait, no flourish in her arrival. Just inevitability.

Her clothes were stained with soot and blood, her face smudged with the remains of war, but her eyes—those eyes—were crystalline with purpose.

They met his, and for a flicker of a second, there was no gun between them, no history heavy with violence—only the brittle silence between a father and daughter at the end of the world.

He laughed. It was a cracked sound, brittle and pitiful. "So this is it, then?" he said, gesturing to the wreckage around them.

"My home. Your inheritance. Look what we've done."

Valentina stopped five feet from him, her hand at her side, resting on the grip of her gun—not in threat, but in promise.

"No," she said. "Look what *you* did."

Marco's shoulders sagged. "I gave you everything. Power. Legacy. I made you strong."

"You made me cruel," she replied, her voice low, unwavering.

"And I thought cruelty was the only way to survive. I became what you molded—and I hated myself for it."

"You're alive because of me," he snapped, desperation creeping in like a stain. "You are *me*."

She tilted her head. "No. That's the lie you told yourself so you could sleep at night."

He took a half-step forward, hand twitching toward the pistol at his hip. It wasn't there. She'd already taken it when he fled through the smoke like a wounded beast. He was unarmed. Unmade.

"You always needed someone to kneel," she said, voice like silk drawn over a blade.

"Someone to break. But you forgot the first rule of kings—eventually, every crown cuts too deep."

"You were my legacy," he whispered, a crack forming in his composure.

"And you killed the only legacy that mattered," she said. "Her."

A flicker of pain crossed his face, but it passed quickly—he had buried sentiment so deep it only surfaced in death. "She was weak."

"No," Valentina said. "She was everything I should've been allowed to be."

The silence between them grew thick, like the pause before thunder. Behind her, the estate burned. Behind him, the vineyard swayed like a field of ash-coated tombstones. The Russo name was dissolving with the wind, one ember at a time.

Marco's knees gave out, and he sank to the dirt, his eyes still locked on hers. "You don't need to do this," he said. "You've already won."

She stepped closer. Not out of pity. Out of clarity. "This was never about winning. This is about *ending* you."

Her hand rose, the gun leveled at his chest. Her finger curled slowly around the trigger. He didn't beg. He wouldn't give her that satisfaction—and she didn't need it.

She wasn't angry anymore.

She was done.

"I chose power," she said softly, the words falling like a ritual. "Then I chose love."

A beat. The world stilled. Even the fire seemed to hush.

"Now, I choose peace."

The shot echoed through the valley like thunder on the edge of a storm. It shattered the quiet, rang across the vineyard, and cracked through the heart of the bloodline.

Marco fell backward into the dirt with his eyes still open—empty, unblinking, devoid of empire or absolution.

Valentina stood over him, unmoving. She didn't flinch. Didn't sigh. Her silence was not numbness—it was resolve. The vineyard didn't weep. It bore witness.

She turned her back on the corpse, her silhouette framed by

the firelight behind her, a crownless queen in black, forged not by inheritance, but by war. The woman who once bled for legacy had buried it in the soil her mother used to tend.

As she walked away, smoke curling around her like a veil, she didn't look back.

There was nothing left to save.

And nothing left to fear.

The past was ash now.

And she wore her hollow crown like armor.

CHAPTER 28

- Aftermath -

THE ESTATE STOOD IN silence, cloaked in the scent of gunpowder and wine. Smoke curled from scorched shutters. Vines bled sap where bullets had torn through them.

The grandeur of the Russo vineyard—the place where it all began, where power was passed like poison through generations—was nothing more than a mausoleum now.

A tomb for legacies, lies, and blood-drenched love stories.

Sunlight strained through a cracked stained-glass window in the chapel, casting fragmented rainbows across the marble floor.

A breeze moved through the corridors like a whisper of all that had been lost.

Footsteps echoed—light, slow, deliberate—along the hallway that once held portraits of ancestors now forgotten.

The frame of Marco Russo's portrait had shattered in the final attack. Only broken glass remained, reflecting a crown no one wanted to inherit.

Valentina moved through the wreckage without a sound. No entourage, no guards, no mask. Just a woman wearing black, barefoot on cold stone, eyes like winter—still and endless.

The war was over. But victory had never been her ambition.

Not really.

She stood before the grave of her mother beneath the old olive tree, where two new headstones had joined it—Ezra, the fallen guardian. Luca, the loyal soldier.

There were no eulogies, no prayers, no priests. Just silence, and a single white rose.

Valentina crouched beside her mother's grave and whispered, "It's done. I didn't win. But I ended it."

The rose fell from her hand, its petals trembling in the breeze.

Time passed, not like a storm, but like snowfall—slow, silent, remorseless.

Gia walked again. Not quickly, not without effort, but each step held defiance. Her body still bore the scars from the Bratva's dungeon, but her eyes had sharpened into something more dangerous than pain: clarity.

Her laughter, rare as it was, returned in fragments. Each one a triumph over the ghosts.

The estate was no longer a fortress. Walls were pulled down. Rooms were gutted. The armory dismantled, piece by piece, until all that remained were open windows and sunlight. In the west wing, papers burned in a stone fireplace—ledgers, names, secrets, blood-money.

The Russo syndicate—once a name that ruled entire nations—was dissolved.

Valentina didn't announce it. She simply acted. She signed over the family's legal businesses to Gia under a new entity: *Fondazione Luce*. A foundation meant to repurpose the fortune built on blood, trafficking, and control into a legacy that could cleanse, not curse. Shelters.

Rehabilitation centers. Intelligence networks for dismantling other operations like theirs.

"Let the name die," she said one evening to Gia. "Let something better live in its place."

Gia looked at her sister, not as a queen, not as a savior, but simply as Valentina. And nodded.

There were no thrones left. Only choices.

The Key

The sea called to her like it always had.

Not the violent waters of Sicily, but the quiet edge of southern France—where cliffs overlooked the turquoise coastline, where no one knew her name, where the wine tasted of sun and time rather than war.

She found the key on her desk one morning. No letter. Just a bronze key on a velvet ribbon and an address scribbled in Damien's familiar hand.

A house with weathered shutters and a fig tree in the yard. No guards. No cameras. Just a door. Waiting to be opened.

He stood in the doorway when she arrived. Said nothing. Just held out his hand.

And for the first time in her life, Valentina didn't think before reaching back.

That night, they didn't speak of empires or endings. They sat beneath the stars with nothing but the hum of cicadas and the soft clink of wine glasses between them. Their fingers touched without demand. Their silence was peace.

He looked at her like she was both flame and water.

She looked at him like he was her only mirror.

"I don't know how to be anything but what I am," she said.

"Then be that. But for you, not them."

No crown. No blood oath. Just breath and possibility.

And so the queen disappeared into the smoke—no longer hunted, no longer hollow. Just a woman with scars, a key, and a second chance.

CHAPTER 29

- Sea Glass & Cigarettes -

THE HOUSE STOOD where the sea met silence—weatherworn stone, white shutters, and a terrace kissed by salt and wind. It was not a fortress, nor a palace. It was something quieter. Older. A place that had waited too long for a woman who might never come.

Damien sat on the terrace every evening, a cigarette burning low between his fingers, his boots kicked up on the railing. The Mediterranean spread before him like bruised glass, the sun collapsing behind it in bleeding streaks of gold.

He'd stopped watching the door. Stopped pretending he could outrun memory or rebuild purpose. He merely waited.

Each night ended with a whisper of her name on his tongue, spoken not as a plea, but as a prayer. A wound still warm.

He'd bought the house in silence, furnished it like a man preparing for someone else's life. In the mornings, he read the paper in French cafés with bitter espresso and no appetite.

At night, he played old jazz on a dusty record player and wondered if peace was a lie they sold to men who survived too much.

No news. No messages. No sign of the woman who had burned down a world and buried her crown in ash. He didn't expect her anymore.

So when the knock came—three slow, deliberate taps against the cedar door—he didn't move.

And then he heard it. The click of bare heels on stone. The hush of breath drawn too carefully. A presence that hadn't belonged to this house until now.

He turned.

And she was there.

Valentina.

Wearing white linen, her hair wind-tossed, her skin sun-kissed and shadowed by old battles. No guards. No mask. No empire following in her wake. Just her. Scarred. Still. Alive.

The silence between them wasn't awkward. It was reverent. He stood slowly, unsure if she'd vanish if he moved too fast.

Her gaze swept the terrace, the sea, the man who hadn't stopped loving her—and then she smiled. Barely. Brokenly. But real.

"You still smoke the French ones," she said, her voice cracked from disuse.

"You still like stealing them," he replied.

And just like that, the world tilted back into place.

Smoke and Sea Glass

They didn't speak much after that. Words would have only thinned the gravity of her return.

She dropped her bag by the door, wandered barefoot across terracotta tiles, and studied the house like it was a memory she hadn't made yet. He followed without needing to follow, their steps synchronized in that old, haunting rhythm that never truly left.

When he reached for her, it wasn't with hunger. It was

reverence. He touched her cheek, his thumb grazing the faint scar below her left eye.

She didn't flinch. Instead, she leaned into his palm and closed her eyes.

"I didn't know if you'd wait," she whispered.

"I didn't know if you'd live," he answered.

That was all they needed.

The rest unraveled like smoke.

He kissed her like he remembered every fight they'd survived and every one they hadn't. She kissed him like she was still trying to forget who she'd had to become.

They stumbled into the walls, into the echo of their own breathing, into the kind of silence that didn't need explanation.

Clothes came off slowly. No urgency. No game. Just hands relearning terrain they'd once bled for.

She cried halfway through—just one tear—but it broke something in him. He kissed the salt from her skin and pressed his forehead to hers.

"Don't you ever leave me again," she said, the words shaking, not from fear, but from the weight of wanting.

He didn't promise. He didn't lie. He simply breathed her name and said, "You'd burn the world before I could."

They didn't stop. Not until they were nothing but raw breath and heat and redemption. Not until the world outside stopped existing.

The Gun on the Nightstand

The morning stretched across the coastline like an old silk slip —quiet, pale, and just a little bruised at the edges.

The sea outside breathed in slow, steady tides, and the world —at least this forgotten corner of it—seemed to hold its breath.

Valentina moved through the bedroom with the stillness of someone no longer hunted, but not yet healed. The white linen shirt hung loosely from her shoulders, swallowing her frame, sleeves rolled to her elbows.

She had taken it from his closet wordlessly that morning, as though reclaiming something long owed.

Sunlight caught the sharp glint of silver at her ankle, the faint echo of a knife scar on her thigh. Her body told the story she never needed to speak. War had etched itself into her skin like scripture.

Damien leaned in the doorway, a mug of coffee in one hand, watching her the way men only watch once they've lost someone and been granted the miracle of their return.

He said nothing. The silence between them had shifted—from tension to reverence. There were no battles left between them now. Only choices.

Valentina crossed the room, barefoot on the cool stone, her hair tangled from sleep and salt air.

She passed by him without a glance, her fingers trailing along the dresser, grazing the lip of a half-open drawer.

She stopped at the nightstand.

And then—gently, decisively—she placed it down.

Her gun.

It was the same Beretta she'd carried since Palermo. Sleek, black, loyal. A weight she had once held like a heartbeat in her palm. The same gun she had used to put down enemies, threaten allies, and protect what little of herself had remained unburnt.

The same one she had once pressed to Damien's ribs in a moment of blurred allegiance.

Now, it lay on his nightstand, its barrel pointed away from the bed. Her fingers lingered on it for a breath longer than necessary.

Not out of hesitation—but farewell.

Damien watched her as if witnessing an eclipse. Not rare. Impossible.

Her voice was low when it came. "I've carried that thing since I was seventeen."

"I know," he said. His throat tightened around the words.

She finally turned toward him. Her eyes weren't watery, but they weren't hard either. They were... unfinished. Open. Like a wound that had decided, at last, to scar.

"I used to sleep with it under my pillow. Now I don't want it near me." She paused. "Not here."

He looked at the gun again—small now, almost pitiful in its loneliness. It had ruled her life for so long. Been her safety. Her curse. Her crown.

"You're sure?" he asked, not because he doubted her, but because it felt like a moment that needed asking.

Valentina nodded, her lips pressing into something that wasn't quite a smile. "If I need to pick it up again, I'll know where it is."

And that was all.

She crossed back to the window and opened it wide, letting the scent of salt, thyme, and citrus wash into the room. Her fingers toyed with a strand of hair, twisting it absentmindedly, like a girl rather than a queen.

Damien placed his coffee down and approached slowly. He didn't touch her. Not yet. Not while she was still balancing on that invisible line between past and present.

"I didn't ask you to stay," he said after a long silence.

"I know."

"You don't have to."

"I know that too."

She turned, the linen shirt billowing slightly as the breeze caught its hem. Her eyes met his, and something between them —something unspeakable and sacred—settled.

"I don't know what forever looks like," she said softly. "But I know what peace feels like now. And I think... I want more of it."

That was enough. It was more than he had ever hoped for.

He stepped forward and wrapped his arms around her waist, pulling her in. She melted into him with the ease of a woman who had earned her rest.

For the first time in years, there was no armor between them.

The gun stayed where she left it, silent and unneeded.

Outside, the sea continued its patient hum.

Inside, two broken people began again—not as weapons, not as ghosts, but as something gentler.

Something real.

CHAPTER 30

- The Queen's Vow -

THE PEN MOVED in slow, deliberate strokes, like a weapon she no longer needed to conceal. Valentina sat at the writing desk in the villa's study, framed by the amber hush of the setting sun. Her fingers, once stained with blood and fury, now bore only a trace of red ink.

The letter she wrote was not an apology. It wasn't a confession, either.

It was something far rarer—a truth uncoiled from the throat of a woman who had survived too much to lie anymore.

The parchment trembled slightly beneath her hand, but the words were steady:

"If I've learned anything... it's that love doesn't make you weak. It makes you want to survive harder. It teaches you how to lose with grace, how to kill without hatred, how to walk away from the fire without needing to watch the world burn with you. I have worn crowns made of glass and knives. I have kissed death and danced with ghosts. But none of them knew how to touch my soul the way you did. And that's what frightened me."

Outside, the sea wind whispered through the open window, carrying salt, memory, and the fading scent of lilac. The empire had long since been dismantled.

Power redistributed. Wars ended. The only revolution left was the one she started in her own chest.

She folded the letter carefully, sealing it with a kiss instead of wax. The Queen of Spades card slipped inside, worn at the corners but still sharp in design.

Her signature, smudged with lipstick, turned it into something sacred.

This wasn't goodbye. This was a reminder.

A promise.

A prophecy.

Roots in the Dust

The vineyard looked nothing like the battlefield it had once been. Where blood had once soaked into the earth, vines now bloomed, thick and stubborn with rebirth.

The old Russo estate had shed its skin and emerged as something softer—no longer a place of syndicate secrets, but a sanctuary lined with green rows, stone paths, and women laughing in the shade of olive trees.

Valentina stood at the edge of the property, her boots dusted in golden soil, her white blouse fluttering like a flag of surrender.

She watched Gia moving among the workers, clipboard in hand, her face radiant beneath the Sicilian sun.

She laughed without flinching. Smiled without fear. When she bent down to speak to a child playing near the vines, something cracked in Valentina's chest—not pain, not sorrow, but awe.

This was what survival looked like when it was allowed to bloom.

She passed beneath the trellis where her mother once taught her how to tie vine knots. At its base now stood a plaque, small and silver:

"Rosalia Russo. She planted us all."

Valentina touched it gently, the same way she'd once touched her mother's grave. There were no tears this time, only peace. For the first time in her life, she didn't need to speak the goodbye aloud.

Because she wasn't leaving.

She was becoming.

The Queen's Game

The letter was not merely a farewell—it was a reckoning, folded into parchment and sealed with a press of scarlet wax.

But the real message came in the form of a card—worn at the edges, the Queen of Spades glinting faintly beneath the soft smudge of crimson lipstick.

Valentina slipped it into the velvet-lined envelope with surgical precision, as though threading a needle through time itself.

Each movement was ritual. Every detail symbolic.

She stood alone in her mother's study, the vineyard humming beyond the windows like a ghost given new breath. The bottle of wine on the table had been poured hours ago, untouched.

The fire in the hearth had long since burned down to embers.

And yet, her presence crackled with energy, a sovereign in exile preparing her next act of war—or rebirth.

Valentina stared at the card one last time before sealing it. Not with nostalgia. Not with longing. But with resolve.

The Queen of Spades—traditionally the card of misfortune and cunning—had become her sigil. A prophecy made flesh.

It was never about vengeance alone. It was about evolution.

She had torn an empire apart, brick by bloody brick. And now, from the wreckage, she had rewritten the blueprint. Women were no longer traded like wine in backroom deals.

Children were no longer trained for loyalty like dogs to a leash. Power was no longer currency—it was sanctuary, and she had redefined its worth.

But part of her knew the calm wouldn't last forever. Peace was a fragile lover, one who never stayed for breakfast. And love—the real, brutal, immortal kind—demanded risk.

She addressed the parcel simply: *D. Moreau*. No return address. No instructions. Just a destination and a dare.

Then she stepped outside, barefoot on the warm stone path, the sky burning orange above the hills. The sun kissed the vines. The earth smelled like rain before the storm. And still, the only sound was her breath—steady, sovereign.

Back inside, the walls echoed with silence. But her scent lingered. Her legacy was carved into the wood, the wine, the very soul of the land.

Somewhere, miles and memories away, Damien would find the envelope.

And when he did, he would understand the message behind the lipstick-kissed Queen.

This isn't over.

This was never a love story.

This was a game.

And she had only just reshuffled the deck.

EPILOGUE

- Let It Burn -

THE GLASS WAS half full. Whiskey as old as his sins shimmered amber under the lamplight, untouched, warming slowly in the curve of his palm. He sat in silence, the letter folded in his lap, edges soft from where his thumb had passed over it again and again, as if her voice could be summoned from ink and parchment alone.

She had written it with no apologies. No promises. Just a kiss pressed to a playing card and a line that tasted like gasoline.

Come find me when you're ready to burn it all again.

He smiled.

Not the kind that touched the eyes. Not softness. No. It was the smile of a wolf who had wandered through fire and come out the other side raw and breathing, the ruin behind him still glowing red.

He reached for the pistol.

The weight of it was familiar. Cold. Righteous. A tool of endings and beginnings. He checked the chamber with muscle memory carved from violence, then set it beside the map.

Her location was circled in red. The ink had bled slightly into the parchment, like a wound refusing to close.

He stood.

Across the room, an old television played in silence. Grainy security footage of the engagement party explosion flickered across the screen.

The chaos. The crimson. Her figure emerging from the smoke, soaked in blood and defiance, a white dress turned war paint. She hadn't waited to be rescued.

She had set the world on fire for him.

And in his darkest hour, when bone met steel and breath clawed from shredded lungs, he'd seen her. Not as a hallucination. Not as a ghost.

But as a vow. Her face—wild, weeping, furious—had become the axis of his survival. She had screamed his name into the smoke of some hell neither of them believed in, and it had kept him tethered.

He hadn't died. Because she wouldn't let him.

Even now, months later, stitched and scarred and dragging breath through iron ribs, he could hear her voice behind his eyelids.

He looked around the room—sparse, silent, sharp. There was nothing left here. No home. No war.

Only her.

He drained the glass, fire sliding down his throat. One last sin for the road.

Then he opened the drawer, pulled out the Queen of Spades she had sent him. Her lipstick was still fresh, like she'd pressed it to the card just hours ago. He slid it into his jacket pocket.

At the door, he paused.

The night beyond was silent. Stars like ice embedded in black silk. A breeze moved through the trees, not soft, but electric.

He said nothing as he stepped into it.

But if someone had been close enough to hear the gravel shift beneath his boots, they might've caught the whisper low in his chest, steady as a war drum.

She rose for me.

Now I rise for her.

The door shut behind him.

Somewhere, far off, something caught flame. It was too early to tell if it was memory or prophecy, but the smoke rose just the same.

He didn't look back.

He lit a cigarette. Loaded his weapon. Started walking toward the inferno.

And with a voice like a knife to velvet, he said—

"Then let it burn."

AFTERWORD

Stories are strange things. They begin in silence—one shadow brushing against another, a name whispered in the dark, a flicker of a heartbeat that refuses to die quietly.

This one began with a girl who wasn't allowed to grieve and a man who wasn't supposed to feel. A queen carved from the ruins of legacy, and a wolf raised by fire.

Forbidden Vows was never about love at first sight. It was about love that survives first betrayal. Then blood. Then death. It was about the kind of loyalty you don't choose—but bleed for.

The kind of power that doesn't corrupt—but awakens. And the kind of woman who walks through hell, not to be saved—but to lead.

Valentina Russo was never created to be tamed. She was born to burn the cage.

And Damien Moreau? He was never the hero. He was the mirror. The match. The reckoning.

Writing their story was never easy. Every chapter pulled from something raw—rage, grief, survival, hunger, hope. There were days I stepped away from the page shaking, unsure if they would make it.

Unsure if *I* would. But they always did. And they didn't come through unscathed. That's the point.

Power is not born—it's reclaimed. Love is not soft—it's armor. And redemption… redemption is earned in ash.

To the readers who walked this entire road with me—thank you. For believing in antiheroes. For understanding broken women. For seeing beauty in violence and poetry in revenge. You didn't just read this book.

You *survived* it with them.

To those who still carry ghosts—may you find your vineyard. Your stillness. Your someone who would burn the world for you.

And if you ever hear a woman whisper: *"Come find me when you're ready to burn it all again"*—

Run toward the fire.

Always,
Nolan Crest

ABOUT THE AUTHOR

Nolan Crest

Nolan Crest writes what haunts him—stories forged in blood, longing, and rebellion. Known for his cinematic prose and emotionally visceral narratives, he crafts dark, slow-burn romances where love is dangerous, survival is seductive, and power is always personal.

With a background in screenwriting and a lifelong obsession with morally complex characters, Nolan blends the grit of crime drama with the poetry of tragic love. His work explores fractured loyalty, psychological warfare, and the kind of devotion that both damns and redeems.

When he's not writing, Nolan is probably drinking too much black coffee, annotating old mafia films, or hunting down forgotten myths that demand to be reborn on the page.

Forbidden Vows is his most personal novel to date—a symphony of vengeance, velvet, and vow-bound hearts.

BOOKS BY THIS AUTHOR

Forbidden Lust

Craving Love

Reckless Love

Untamed Passion

Wild Obsession

Irresistible Heat

Bound By Midnight

Sorcerer's Kiss

Whispers Of Temptation

Into His Arms

Made in United States
Troutdale, OR
05/07/2025